ALWAYS WATCH YOUR BACK

My five-story concrete building stands across from a movie house. There's a low-slung shopping mall on one side of it. New high rises all around. I pushed into the foyer. Picked up my mail. Got into the tiny elevator. Leaned back against the wall as the doors closed.

I was more tired than I thought. I shut my eyes. I smiled to myself. Tom Watts, I thought. I had him.

When the door opened, I propelled myself into the hall. Down the hall to my door. I unlocked it, pushed against it with my shoulder.

I came into the familiar semidark. The lights from the street. The red glow of the movie marquee. The cracks on the wall.

I closed the door behind me. I reached for the light switch.

And someone looped a cord around my neck, and pulled it taut.

Bantam Crime Line Books offer the finest in classic and modern American murder mysteries.
Ask your bookseller for the books you have missed.

Rex Stout

Broken Vase
Death of a Dude
Death Times Three
Fer-de-Lance
The Final Deduction
Gambit
The Rubber Band
Too Many Cooks
The Black Mountain
Plot It Yourself
Three for the Chair

Max Allan Collins

The Dark City
Bullet Proof

A. E. Maxwell

Just Another Day in Paradise
Gatsby's Vineyard
The Frog and the Scorpion
Just Enough Light to Kill

Loren Estleman

Peeper

Mary Jo Adamson

Not Till a Hot January
A February Face
Remember March
April When They Woo
May's Newfangled Mirth

Dick Lupoff

The Comic Book Killer

Randy Russell

Hot Wire

V. S. Anderson

Blood Lies

William Murray

When The Fat Man Sings
The King of the Nightcap

Eugene Izzi

King of the Hustlers

Gloria Dank

Friends Till the End

Robert Goldsborough

Murder in E Minor
Death on Deadline
The Bloodied Ivy
coming soon: The Last Coincidence

Sue Grafton

"A" Is for Alibi
"B" Is for Burglar
"C" Is for Corpse
"D" Is for Deadbeat
"E" Is for Evidence

Richard Hilary

Snake in the Grasses
Pieces of Cream
Pillow of the Community
Behind the Fact

Carolyn G. Hart

Design for Murder
Death on Demand
Something Wicked
Honeymoon With Murder
coming soon: A Little Class on Murder

Annette Meyers

The Big Killing

Rob Kantner

Dirty Work
The Back-Door Man
Hell's Only Half Full

Robert Crais

The Monkey's Raincoat
Stalking the Angel

Keith Peterson

The Trapdoor
There Fell a Shadow
The Rain
Rough Justice

David Handler

The Man Who Died Laughing
The Man Who Lived by Night

Jeffery Deaver

Manhattan Is My Beat

ROUGH JUSTICE

Keith Peterson

BANTAM BOOKS
NEW YORK · TORONTO · LONDON · SYDNEY · AUCKLAND

ROUGH JUSTICE
A Bantam Book / November 1989

ISBN 0-553-28297-2

Published simultaneously in the United States and Canada

Bantam Books are published by Bantam Books, a division
of Bantam Doubleday Dell Publishing Group, Inc. Its trademark, consisting of the words "Bantam Books" and the
portrayal of a rooster, is Registered in U.S. Patent and
Trademark Office and in other countries. Marca Registrada.
Bantam Books, 666 Fifth Avenue, New York, New York 10103.

PRINTED IN THE UNITED STATES OF AMERICA

KR   0 9 8 7 6 5 4 3 2 1

THIS BOOK IS FOR FAITH

Prologue

In Little Italy, on the corner of Mulberry Street and Hester, there's a public school. It's a brick building, three stories high. In the top two stories there are classrooms. Lots of little kids with wide eyes. A is for Apple. Two plus two. Under that, on the bottom floor, there are offices, a small auditorium, and a gym. At various times during the day, the kids come downstairs and play in the gym. Kickball, Dodgeball, Red Rover, Red Rover. On warm days, the kids can play in the courtyard just outside. It's a small yard, maybe fifteen by twenty. There are monkey bars and a swing set in it. Under the monkey bars and the swing set, there's a layer of rubber padding. Under the rubber padding, there's a layer of cement. Under the cement, there is E.J. McMahon.

A couple of decades ago—in what you might call his airier days—E.J. was a restaurateur. Easy E.J., they called him then. He had a little steak house in Brooklyn. A family place. The Conti family was especially fond of it. Members of the Conti family liked to sit around E.J.'s of an evening, swallowing prime cuts and chewing over the family business.

1

The family business included extortion, loan sharking, hijacking, and car theft. Stuff like that.

One of the family's more impressive members was an up-and-coming crew chief named Dellacroce. Later on, Dellacroce would become what tabloid reporters like me call a "reputed crime czar." But back then—back when E.J. was still on top of the cement—Dellacroce worked for Conti. Ripping off airport cargo, collecting loans, killing people. Stuff like that.

Now, Easy E.J. McMahon enjoyed playing the ponies. He would place his bets by phone with one of the bookies in Dellacroce's crew. He would place his first bet on Wednesday each week, and his last bet each week on Monday. On Tuesday, he would settle up, win or lose. Unfortunately, for E.J. there finally came a Tuesday when settling up was not so easy. It had something to do with a big bet on a filly named Jiffy McGee. The bet was supposed to pull him even for the month. But while Jiffy may have been a McGee, she wasn't all that Jiffy. E.J. dropped a dime on her, which left him out a total of some twenty K.

E.J. did not have twenty K. In fact, if the J hadn't stood for Jack, he wouldn't have had a K to his name. So he had to borrow the money from one of Dellacroce's sharks. Twenty K with vigorish—interest. Interest of about 200 percent. To make a long story short, this is how Dellacroce came to be the principal owner of E.J. McMahon's Steak House.

Today, Dellacroce's morals are matched only by his charm. He was no different then. He was quick to make sure that E.J. understood his new position in the business. He snapped his fingers at him whenever he wanted something. He barked at him across the room. He even slapped him in the face once when E.J. brought him the wrong kind of potatoes.

Poor E.J. He had never aspired to being much more than a mob toady, but he had his pride. He began to harbor a certain resentment toward Dellacroce. So right off, you might say, he had one foot in the cement.

E.J. nursed his resentment for several years. There then came what he saw as his opportunity for revenge.

At that time, Conti's star had gone into the decline. He was in poor health, and the feds were badgering him with one indictment after another. Dellacroce, on the other hand, had begun to gather numerous admirers and adherents. Seizing the opportunity, Dellacroce went to the city's four other bosses and politely asked permission to have Conti's brains blown out. Permission was granted.

But it was not going to be an easy hit. Conti knew something was up and so his security was tight. He rarely left his Long Island house, and the place was like a fortress. Guards, fences, dogs, the whole thing. Sometime within the next week or so, Dellacroce dined on steak in the back room of E.J.'s Steak House. While he dined, he discussed these matters with a compatriot.

E.J. was hurrying to bring his employer more wine when he overheard the discussion

Now, E.J. did not much care what happened to Sam Conti. But he did think it would be amusing if Dellacroce were riddled with bullets, dumped in a barrel of lime, and tossed into the Hudson River. So off the former restaurateur rushed to Conti's fortresslike home. There, he pleaded urgently with various underlings until he managed to get a hearing from the boss himself.

I must speak to you alone, Don Conti, E.J. said— or words to that effect.

What is it, my friend? said the Don, who loved what E.J. could do with ground round.

For your own safety, I must insist that we are alone, Don Conti, said E.J.

And I, for my own safety, must insist on a bodyguard, said Don Conti. *For I fear there is foul play afoot.* Or words to that effect.

Anyway, the Don dismissed his consigliere and his underboss. But his personal bodyguard continued to stand massively just within the doorway.

Now, said the Don, *what is it, my son?*

Godfather, said E.J. (Well, I wasn't there: he could have said it.) *Godfather, I fear the notorious Dellacroce has won sanction to murder you.*

What? Conti said. *Not Dellacroce, whom I have nursed in my bosom like a son.*

The very same, said E.J., his voice solemn, his grin inward.

Pale, Conti shook his head. He waved his hand in dismissal. *Thank you, my friend, I must be alone now,* he said.

And E.J. bowed, backed out of the room, and drove back to Brooklyn, a happy man.

So anyway, it came to pass that, when Dellacroce's hit men arrived at Conti's house that night, Conti's bodyguard was expecting them.

Oh, hello, said the bodyguard, *I've been expecting you. Mr. Conti is in the study. Go right in.* Or words to that effect.

Conti's body was discovered the next morning, his face on his desk, his brains on the wall behind him.

The slaughter of a mob boss in his own home was a spectacular feat. It required incredible planning, almost impossible control. Most of all, it required the corruption of Conti's closest friends and his personal bodyguard. If Dellacroce's star had been on the rise before, it was now burning like the sun.

E.J. McMahon's star, however, had fallen from the heavens like Lucifer. Thus, when E.J. heard of Mr. Conti's demise, he decided to remove himself from the vicinity. Unfortunately, like the horse he'd bet on, he was not quite jiffy enough.

E.J. planned his escape well. He figured if he could keep to main thoroughfares and crowded places, he would be all right. Dellacroce was unlikely to risk a public shoot-out just to bump off a loudmouth waiter. That's what he figured, anyway.

And, at first, it worked. He got to the bank. That was good. He had a small savings account there, and he cleared it out. No trouble. He even made it to Kennedy Airport. And it was busy. And he was glad.

He bought a one-way ticket to Cheyenne, Wyoming. He thought he might like it there. He started walking from the ticket counter toward the gate.

Two large men in two dark suits stepped out of the crowd. They stood in front of him.

E. J. McMahon? said one of the men. *You are under arrest.*

E.J. was no fool. *You're not cops*, he said.

Yes we are, said the men. *And you are under arrest. Please come with us.*

You're not cops, said E.J. *If you are cops, let's see your badges.*

Both large men reached into their dark suits. Both pulled out police tins. They showed them to E.J.

What? said E.J.

The two men took hold of his arms.

E.J. started to scream. *These guys are not cops. Help. Police.* Or words to that effect.

Right away, airport police came running from all directions. They surrounded the men who were holding E.J. They demanded to see their identification. Once again, the two men reached into their suits and produced their badges.

The airport cops studied the badges carefully. Then they handed the badges back to the two men. Then they nodded their approval. Then the two men took E.J. away.

But they're not cops, E.J. kept screaming.

The two men took him outside. There was a car waiting at the curb. They hustled E.J. into the back seat.

They're not cops, E.J. screamed up at the evening sky.

One man climbed into the back seat with E.J. The other man got in front behind the wheel. The doors of the car closed. The car drove away.

E.J. was never seen again. Not by the public anyway. Not by the cocktail waitress he lived with either. Or by her kid. Or by anyone who ever let on.

Officially, the last thing anyone saw of him, he was being hustled into that car. The last thing anyone heard him say was: *They're not cops. They're not cops.*

So it is obvious that E.J. was not a very bright fellow. He did a lot of things wrong. He was wrong to lose twenty thousand dollars. He was wrong to bet on Jiffy McGee. He was wrong to hold a grudge against a tough guy like Dellacroce. And he was wrong to try a double cross at the upper levels of the mob.

As it turns out, he was also wrong about those two guys who took him out of the airport. He was wrong about their not being cops. That's exactly what they were.

I found that out some fifteen years later.

1

It was on a Tuesday in May, to be exact. I got home from the paper early. I'd just finished up a series on Cable TV graft. We had a new managing editor starting tomorrow. Everything was in waiting, nothing was cooking. The Mets were on free TV. I took the night off.

I got back to my place on Eighty-sixth Street around 8:00. I picked up my mail and went upstairs. The apartment was dark, but I could make out the cracks on the wall. The harsh light from the shops on the street came in through the window. So did a red glow from the Triplex marquee. And the traffic noise. And a spring breeze.

I went to the refrigerator first, got a beer. I went into the bedroom second, switched on the TV. I dropped into my easy chair, loosened my tie, lit a cigarette. I went through the mail, half-listening to the pre-game chatter.

I tore open an envelope, watching the lineups on the set. It was New York against L.A.

Life is good, I thought.

The phone rang.

Shit, I thought.

9

I tossed my mail on the bed, picked up the phone. I was still watching the tube.

A hoarse whisper came over the line. "Wells? John Wells?"

"Yeah."

"This is Sergeant Frank D'Angelo."

"Yeah?"

"You know me."

I considered it. "No, I don't."

"I'm dying," he said.

"I still don't know you, pal."

"Yeah, you do. Sure you do."

"Do I? Maybe I do."

"Yeah." He coughed. "The desk sergeant at the 112th."

"Oh yeah. Oh yeah, sure. Sure I know you." I heard him cough again. "So you're dying, huh?"

"Yeah."

"That's too bad. That's rough."

"Lung cancer."

"That's really too bad, Frank." I put out my cigarette.

"Wells," he gasped. "I need to see you."

"Uh, now?" Orel Hershiser was pitching for L.A.

"Yeah," said Sergeant D'Angelo. "I'm down at St. Vincent's. Could you come down?"

"St. Vincent's, huh?" Against Doc Gooden for the Mets.

"Yeah. Yeah, I gotta talk to you, Wells. I ain't got much time."

Doc Gooden, Frank, I thought. *Don't they rent out TV's at St. Vincent's?* "Sure," I said. "Sure, Frank, I'll come right down."

"Thanks, John. I appreciate it."

"Sure," I said. *Life is shit,* I thought.

And it wasn't any picnic getting to St. Vincent's either. It was way the hell downtown. I had to take the Six train to Fourteenth and then change over. It was probably the third inning just by the time I got there.

When I did get there, I found Frank D'Angelo. He was lying in a bed in a room on the fourth floor. He was dying, all right. He looked all shrunken and gray. I couldn't exactly remember what he looked like before, but not all shrunken and gray, I'm sure of it. The flesh was hanging from his cheeks. His eyes bulged—they were bright as lanterns. He had just a few strands of hair stretched over his spotted pate. Under his pale blue pajamas, a thin frame fought for breath. He wheezed, he snorted, he grunted. He lifted a skeletal hand in the air and waved at me to close the door. I closed it. He waved at me to sit down.

It was a semiprivate room but the other bed was empty. I sat on the edge of it.

"You look good, Frank," I said.

"It's bad, John. It's real bad."

I nodded. "Yeah."

He tried to smile. "Don't smoke," he gasped.

"Nah. I gave it up years ago."

"Yeah, give it up, because this... this is bad."

I nodded. I looked away from him. I looked at the green walls. I looked at the print of hunting dogs on the wall across from him. I looked at the small window on the wall beside him. There was a view of a bunch of water towers atop downtown roofs. I listened to him wheeze and gasp. I nodded.

"Nice view," I said.

"Yeah. They treat you nice here."

"That's good."

"Real nice."

"That's good, Frank."

"Yeah."

"They don't give you a TV?"

"Yeah. Yeah, I got a TV."

"Oh."

"But I been thinking."

"Yeah?"

"You know. About things."

"Oh. Yeah. Sure."

"I guess I never shoulda let my wife go. Take the kids."

I nodded. "Yeah. Great girl."

"Betty."

"Betty, right. Terrific lady."

He rose up a little and coughed hard. A streak of spittle went down one corner of his mouth. "Oh God," he gasped.

"You okay?"

"Yeah, yeah." He fought for another breath. "You're divorced too, right, John?"

"Yeah."

"You got kids?"

"No. Well . . . she died."

"Oh yeah, I remember," he gasped. "Killed herself, right?"

"Yeah."

"I remember hearing. That's a shame." He lay back flat. He stared up at the ceiling with his bright eyes. "It's bad," he said. "Not to have anybody. Now, you know. The end. Betty gone. The kids, they don't even know me. Live out west. My oldest girl, she called a few times. She don't know me. No one to visit. You lie here. You make these noises. You try to breathe. You get to thinking."

I kept nodding. "You oughta get your mind off it, Frank," I said. "Watch TV or something. Sports. You know, it's baseball season."

"Yeah. Yeah. But I been thinking, ya know. I been thinking about E. J. McMahon." He turned his head on his pillow. He gazed at me. "You remember E.J.?"

I thought about it, shrugged. "No, I don't . . ."

"Easy E.J.," he said.

"Oh yeah," I said. "Yeah. The steak house guy, yeah. Tried to tip off Conti before the Long Island hit. I've heard that story from a couple of guys, that's a good story. It happened a few years before I came to the *Star*."

"Remember how he disappeared . . . ?"

"Right out of the airport. Two guys posing as cops." I snorted. "Poor idiot."

"Yeah," Sergeant Frank D'Angelo wheezed. "E. J. McMahon was an idiot."

"I'll say."

"But those guys weren't posing as cops."

I chewed that over. I patted the cigarettes in my shirt pocket. I was beginning to get the urge. "They weren't? That's what I heard. Posing as cops, yeah, that was it."

"I mean, they weren't posing, Wells. They were cops, I mean. They were really cops."

My hand fell away from my shirt pocket. I almost said something. Then I didn't. I sat on the edge of the empty bed. I watched the man's sagging gullet work each breath over. I watched the cloth of his pajama top shudder.

"You," I said.

He frowned. His lips trembled. A tear spilled out of one eye. It ran into his crow's-feet, worked its way through the map of crevices on his face, dripped onto his pillow. He had to take an enormous gasp for air, and he coughed it back out again.

Goddamn it, I thought. It was a good story. A very good story. But I did not want a good story right then. I wanted to go home. I wanted to watch the Mets.

"My partner brought it to me," Frank D'Angelo whispered. "A favor for some guys, he said. Wiseguys, but okay, he said. Good money in it." He shifted his head a little so he could look at me. Look at me with those burning eyes. "We were plainclothes, then, you know. We were way on the pad, deep on. It seemed like just another thing, you know. That's what he said it was, my partner. Just another thing. A favor."

I took a breath, tried to keep steady. I wanted a cigarette bad now.

"You know. . ." He faltered. A strange sound came out of his chest. "You know that school, that kid's school. On Mulberry Street."

I shook my head. "I guess. Sure."

"That's where we took him. E.J.—" He fought back a coughing fit. "They were building it then. Making a sort of yard, like a. . . like a playground. Filling in the foundation. A dump truck. . . They had a dump truck there. Rough stone in it, you know. Like gravel, only big. Big pieces of gravel."

"Who? Who had them?"

"Four guys. Wiseguy types. Muscle. They were waiting for us. I didn't know them."

"Okay," I said.

"Yeah. So they took E.J. out of the car. And E.J. started screaming. So one of the guys stuffed a rubber ball in his mouth. Taped it shut. One of the other guys, he says to me, 'You wanna watch this?' He's laughing. 'This is gonna be good,' he says. 'Hang around and watch this.'" Sergeant Frank D'Angelo's whole body shook. "I didn't want to. I didn't want to know about it, you know? But my partner, he got all excited. 'Let's hang around,' he said. 'Let's hang around and watch.' I figured they were gonna, you know, bust him up a little."

I rubbed a hand over my face. I'd begun to sweat. "Hot in here," I muttered. My lungs were working hard, really itching for that smoke.

"They tied him up," Frank rasped. "E.J. They tied him up, hands and feet so he couldn't stand, he just could lie there. Then they tossed him into the hole, the foundation hole. It went down. It was deep. And there was a big construction fence there so no one could see from the street. But the people in the other buildings—some of them . . . They must've seen. Some of them."

"Wait a minute," I said.

"Then they backed up the dump truck . . ."

"Wait a minute, didn't they shoot him?"

A second tear spilled down that wasted face.

"Didn't they shoot him?" I said.

"They said, 'Wait around and watch this.' They said, 'This is gonna be funny.' They just backed up the truck and dumped the gravel over him. He was still alive, Wells. They poured the gravel over him. Slow-like. I could see his face for a long time. I could see him thrashing around. Then after . . . after he was all covered . . ." He stopped for a second, but he didn't cough. He hardly breathed. ". . . you could just see the gravel shifting. Moving, you know, with him under."

"Jesus."

"Moving around."

"Jesus."

"And they were all laughing. One of em said . . . I remember, he said, 'We're gonna have to use a compactor. Keep the concrete from sagging when he rots.' They were laughing." Now the coughing burst from him. It was damp and deep. He lifted his head off the pillow. His face went purple. The phlegm boiled in his chest.

"You all right?" I said.

He kept coughing.

I got up from the bed. "Frank?"

D'Angelo rolled over onto his side. His hand went out toward the call button.

I rushed to the door. Pushed out into the hall. The nurse's station was only a few steps away. Several people in white were milling behind the counter.

"Hey, we need help here!" I said.

At once, two people ran around the counter. A nurse in white, a young man—an intern—in blue. I could hear Frank hacking and gasping behind me. The nurse and the intern ran past me. They went to him.

When I turned back into the room, they were hovering over him.

"You'll have to go," the intern said. He didn't look up.

I nodded. I started to turn.

A hand shot out between the intern and the nurse. A skeletal hand, stretched out toward me. I stopped.

"You'll have to go!" the intern ordered.

But I didn't go. I walked over and stood beside them. The nurse was holding a mask over Frank's face. The doctor was giving him some kind of shot. Frank was taking deep, shuddering breaths. His eyes stared and stared at me over the mask.

He reached up toward me with one hand. With the other, he knocked at the mask weakly.

"We have to take him downstairs," the intern said. He looked scared. He must have been twenty-five.

"He wants to say something," I said.

"Get out of here," he said to me. Then he said to the nurse: "Get the resident. We're gonna have to

take him downstairs. Get out of here!" he said to me
again.

The nurse rushed out of the room. The mask was
strapped to Frank's face.

"You're going to be okay," the intern said.

Frank reached up and took the mask off. His face
was slack, his bright eyes dimming.

"Partner..." he said.

The intern grabbed the mask.

"Yeah," I said. "Yeah. Who was your partner?"

The intern moved frantically to put the mask back
over the dying man's face. Just before he did, though,
Frank D'Angelo whispered: "Tom Watts."

2

At nine sharp the next morning, I walked into the *Star*'s city room whistling a jolly tune.

Rafferty, the city editor, raised his grizzled, bullet-shaped head from his computer terminal.

"Nice day," I said.

Various editors around the long desk froze. They looked up at me.

I stopped just inside the glass doors. "What?" I said.

Rafferty's imperturbable voice squeezed out between his unmoving lips. "Nice day?"

"Yeah." The editors stared at me. "You know: blue skies, singing birds."

"You actually heard these birds?"

"Well, no, but—it's spring. There must be birds." I stared back at them. "I mean, it's May. New York is at its best in May."

"Paris is at its best in May," muttered Jones, a wire editor. "It's Autumn in New York."

"Has all the thrill of first nighting," Rafferty said.

"Oh. Yeah. Well, anyway..." I stuck a cigarette between my teeth. Lit it. I jogged my eyebrows over the smoke. "It's still a nice day."

"All right," Rafferty muttered. "All right, what have you got? In a word or less."

"In a word or less? Watts," I said.

The editors standing around the desk permitted themselves a soft murmur.

Even Rafferty almost reacted. "You got Watts?" he said.

"I got lots of Watts. I got all the Watts there is to gots."

The assistant city editor, Vicki Goldblum, sat perched on the edge of the desk. "Well, what do you know? That might just save you from the wrath of your new boss."

"The thought had crossed my mind," I said. "Speaking of which, is my new boss here?"

Rafferty made a vague gesture toward the ceiling. "With the People Upstairs. They're discussing something about giving you a party... a going-away party... a retirement party..."

"A necktie party, I think it was," said Vicki.

"Something like that," Rafferty said. "They ought to be down soon."

I took a long, sweet drag of my cigarette. "Well," I said. "It's still a nice day. Still." And I left them there.

I walked into the maze of cubicles that stretches over the vast white room. I heard the hum of computer keyboards, the soft murmur of voices rising over the white walls, under the rows of fluorescent lights. I came to my own space. Stood staring a second at the debris on my desktop. Finally, I shoved a pile of newspapers to one side. They splattered onto the floor. Where they had been, there was now revealed an old Olympia Standard typewriter. I sat down in front of it. Found a piece of paper under an old Big Mac carton. I tossed the carton in the trash. I rolled the page into the machine.

I pulled a notebook from my pocket. Flipped it open. The pages were almost full. There were also some torn and crumpled slips that fell out onto the desk. Some of them were stained or smeared. They still smelled of Scotch.

I never did get to see the Mets last night. I never even got to read my mail. I sat at the desk in my apartment until three in the morning. I sipped liquor and smoked and wrote down what Frank D'Angelo had told me. Then I dug out some of my old clips on Tom Watts. I read through them, taking notes, sipping Scotch, smoking. Then, smoking and sipping Scotch, I wrote down the names of everyone I would want to call. Then I stumbled into the bedroom through a haze of cigarette smoke. Then I dropped facedown onto the unmade bed. Then I woke up, took off my clothes, put on some other clothes and came to work.

Now, I started typing up some of my notes. I also started to scream at the top of my lungs: "Fran!" I kept on typing.

A small voice called back at me: "What?"

I stopped typing. "*What?*" I said. I stood up, looked over my cubicle wall.

Fran was at her computer terminal at an open desk at the front of the city room. She was peering at the monitor. Her long black hair was tied back severely. Her monkey face was set and grim.

"Fran," I explained—still at the top of my lungs. "Fran, not 'What?' More like: 'Here's your coffee, Mr. Wells. Black, just the way you like it. Mm mm.' And, Fran—try to sound subservient." She let out an angry breath at her screen and started to stand. I sat back down. "*What!*" I muttered. I went on with my typing.

Two voices, male and female, started up behind me.

"Have you noticed," said the man, "that ever since Cambridge was canned, there's been a certain—I don't know..."

"Spring in his step?"

"A lilt, I'd call it."

"A lilt in his voice, you mean."

"A lilt in his voice, a spring in his step."

"A gleam in his eye."

"A song in his heart."

"A pain in my ass," I said, swiveling around.

Lansing was sitting on the file cabinet to my left. She was eating a buttered hard roll. McKay was leaning against the partition to my right. He was drinking coffee from a Styrofoam cup.

"So what do we figure it's gonna be now?" McKay asked no one in particular. The fat cheeks of his baby face curled with a smile. "Likability. Predictability."

I lit a fresh cigarette and leaned back in my chair. "With the new boss, you mean?"

McKay sipped his coffee. "Yeah, I mean, now that Cambridge is gone, and we don't have to be relatable

anymore." He sighed. "I'll miss that. The *Star* won't
be the same without it. No more relatability. No
more infotainment. You know, I think I'll miss
infotainment most of all."

"Don't count on it," said Lansing. She tossed back
her blond hair. Nibbled at her roll. "It's always
something. It was something before Cambridge.
Weren't we zingy once?"

"I was zingy," I said. "You weren't born."

"I hear you weren't that zingy."

"Gimme a piece of your roll."

"Here you are, Mr. Wells. Brown. Just the way
you like it."

" Mm mm," I said. I took the roll, looking up into
her face. Into the blue eyes in her porcelain oval of a
face and then down over the long lean body in the
trim white skirt suit, the long white legs crossed at
the knee. I looked away. I ate the roll. She's too
young for me. She's twelve. I'm a million.

"So," McKay said. "I hear you're in Dutch with
our new leader even before we have a new leader."

"That's the word I get too."

"Here's your coffee, Mr. Wells." It was Fran. She
was sneering. She jutted a Styro at me. "Enjoy it
while you can."

"Mm mm," I said. "Black. Just the way I like it."

She spun a bunch of plaid pleats at me and stomped
away.

"What's wrong with her?" I said.

"What do they want from you anyway?" said Lansing.
"You had us on top of the Abingdon story all through
the election."

"Right," said McKay. "Exactly. That made Cambridge look so bad, we lost our last ounce of respect for him."

"We had an ounce?" I said.

"So they fire him and now it looks like Wells is more powerful than the managing editor. So now they have to cut him down to size. Management Technique One-A."

"You didn't happen to hear any specific points of this plan?" I asked. "Am I gonna be put on obits or something?"

He shook his head. "They don't tell me their secret thoughts. Something about opera reviews, though."

"Great. How about the boss? What's the rundown?"

"Not good."

"Tell all."

"You won't like it."

"Come on."

"Advertising."

"No, really."

"Sorry, Wells."

"Oh boy."

"Rich. Father owns a chain of papers based in Texas. Ivy League. Princeton, I think. Columbia J school. Some kind of trainee job on a little paper up in Schoharie. Then—the hungry weeks of struggling over at last—on to Madison Avenue. Sheckner and Covey."

"The guys who did the Gordon campaign."

"And Dog Bits. 'He'll thank you for 'em.'"

"Christ."

Fran returned. She was not sneering. She was smiling. She curtsied at me. Her eyes gleamed.

"Your presence is requested in the managing editor's office, Mr. Wells." And off she flounced.

"Uh—shit?" I said.

"Sounds about right to me," said McKay.

I stood up. Lansing swallowed the last of her roll and slid down off the cabinet. Her fingers were long and white, too, like her legs. She fixed my tie with them. She smelled of lilacs.

"Think of me from time to time—and smile," I told her.

"You're the best they've got," she said. "What can they do to you?"

I patted her shoulder. "No matter what, we'll always have Paris."

"We never had Paris."

"Too bad. She's at her best in May."

I saluted and started down the hall toward manager's row.

3

She had gray eyes and orders to break my back. Her name was Emma Walsh.

She was standing at her window when I came in. The window looked out over Vanderbilt Avenue. She turned to me when I closed the door. She stood framed against the silver of the Pan Am Building.

She smiled. "John Wells," she said. Her lips were very full, her lipstick very red. She was about my age—forty-six—but the skin of her round face was smooth, and her gray eyes glittered. She wore her brown hair long down her back like a girl. She was compact and full-figured. Her breasts made her red sweater swell. Her hips pressed against her gray skirt.

She held her hand out and took a stride toward me. I met her, shook her hand. A small, soft hand.

"I wanted to meet you as soon as I could," she said. "Seeing as I have a mandate to crush you."

"So I hear."

She smiled again. She had to draw her hand back to get it away from me. I managed to hold her eyes another second before she turned away. Then I watched her gray skirt sway as she walked behind her desk. She sat down, gestured me to the seat in front of her.

"You can smoke if you want."

"Thanks." I lit up.

"I understand that's been something of a sore point. Smoking."

"Cambridge thought it was bad for my health. He was only thinking of me."

She sat back in her swivel chair. It was the big kind with the high back, the executive kind. The office was the executive model, too. Spacious, with a solid oak desk. Two leather chairs in front of it. A sofa against the opposite wall. There were no pictures. Cambridge had never hung any. It sped things up when he cleaned the place out, anyway.

"I understand there've been a lot of sore points around here," she said.

"A few."

"Cambridge and you didn't get along."

I waved my cigarette in the air. "We had some differences of opinion."

"Like Hitler and Churchill?"

"That would be a fair comparison, yeah."

"Okay." She motioned at me. "What's your version?"

I let out a breath of smoke, sat back in the chair. I eyed her. She eyed me back, steadily.

"He wanted me to learn the computers," I said after a while. "I like my typewriter. He didn't want me to put my feet on my desk. I wanted to."

Emma Walsh pursed her red lips. She did not look happy. I tried again.

"Also, he wanted to save the front page for beauty

pageants and rock stars, and I kept writing stuff about crooks on the public payroll, politicians with organized-crime connections, that kind of thing. He was a thirty-year-old executive. I'm forty-six, and still covering the street. He thought he must know something to be dressed so well. Finally, I turned down a chance to break a sex scandal on a Senate candidate, and we got scooped. He bet his reputation he could make me look bad for it." I shrugged. "He lost."

There was a long silence. She brushed her hair back with her hand. I watched her do it. Her hair looked very soft. "So why do they hate you?" she asked. "The People Upstairs."

I shrugged again. "They hired an idiot. I made him look like an idiot."

"And now they've hired someone from an advertising firm."

"At least you've heard of Winston Churchill."

She startled me with a laugh. It was a rich, high, musical sound. Her gray eyes grew even brighter. She nodded. "Poor Mr. Cambridge. I pity him. I do." She had just the softest trace of a southern accent. You had to listen for it. "All right, let me tell you what I've been hearing this past week or so."

I took a deep breath. "Go ahead."

"You'll be relieved to know: I haven't been brought here like Cambridge was, to make the *Star* relatable."

"Good."

"Or zingy like Perelman."

"Fine."

"Or even to give it pizzazz..."

"Like Davis, yeah, I remember him."

"They want me to make it perky," said Emma Walsh.

"Uh..."

"Like my dog-food commercials."

"They'll thank you for it."

"That's the one."

"Well, then, Miss Walsh," I said after a moment, "I'm sure dog owners will soon be buying this paper, too."

She twisted her mouth at me, nodded. Pointed a slick red fingernail at me. "And I was warned about you, my friend."

"Me? No kidding. Little Jacky Wells?"

" 'The minute you get any trouble from *him*,' they told me. 'The very *instant*. You come down on him and come down hard. Bury his stuff if you have to. Reassign him. But...' " Now she held the finger in the air. " 'But...' "

"I can't stand the suspense."

" 'But don't let him get away.' That's what they said to me. The People Upstairs. I'm quoting. 'Don't let him quit and go to the *News* because then they'll beat everybody out on metro stuff instead of us.' So what I want to ask you is: How can I break your spirit without making you quit?"

"Drugs?"

"I thought of that. I don't have the budget line."

She let out that laugh again. Lifting her chin, baring her throat. I used the moment to run my eyes down over her. Then she stopped laughing and I stopped looking. I put out my cigarette in the ashtray on her desk. Pulled a fresh one out of my pocket quickly.

"You know, you *are* going to hurt yourself with those one of... Okay, okay. I'm not saying anything."

I lit the cigarette. When I glanced up at her through the smoke, she was studying me. She was not smiling anymore. I couldn't read her eyes.

"So who else have I got out there?" she asked me.

"You asking me to name troublemakers?"

"I'm asking you who else is good."

I pretended to think it over while I tried to get her number. I still wasn't sure where she'd come down. But I said, "Lansing, definitely."

"You helped bring her on here, right?"

"She's good, for all that. She'd walk into a fire to get you react from a dying child."

"And you pal around with that boy McKay, don't you?"

"Yeah, but he's our Shakespeare."

"Homeless Mother Gets Job? Sick Kid Finds Lost Dog?"

"Struggling Actor with AIDS, right. He's tops with that stuff."

"Never a dry eye."

"I think he even read a book once."

"Okay," she murmured. "Okay." She sat back in her chair, considered all this awhile. Tapped a pencil against her bottom lip. Nodded to herself.

I rolled my cigarette in my fingers for something to do. Watched the ember turning. Told myself not to sweat. Sweat.

"My older brother was named Ned," said Emma

Walsh. "Edward. We called him Ned. One day, when he was sixteen, my daddy sent him out to the garage to start up the car. The car blew up and killed him."

For a second, I just sat there. Looking at her. Wearing a face so stupid you could have bought it in a Times Square novelty shop. Finally, I managed to say, "Jeez. That's tough."

"Yeah. It's tough, all right."

"It was meant for your father."

"He owned a chain of papers. They were on a campaign against the governor, exposing his links with the mob."

"Robert Walsh," I said. "Your old man's Robert Walsh."

"That's right."

"I didn't get that. I didn't make the connection."

She leaned forward again and the light played over her hair. When she smiled now, I could make out the laugh lines around her mouth. And the steely glint in the gray eyes. She was smart, I could tell. She was smarter than me. A bad thing in a boss. It made me nervous. "I studied English literature at Princeton. You probably know all this. Journalism at Columbia?"

"I've heard it around," I said.

"When I graduated, I got a job on a little paper called the *Wallkill Record*. All by myself, no connections. I was very proud." One corner of her mouth lifted. She held me with that gaze. "I covered church meetings, barbecues. Town board twice a month. And after half a year, the editor—very sweet guy by the name of Porky Hindenburg—he sat down on my desk, put his fatherly hand on my shoulder, and said,

'Emma, you're going to have a long and happy career. Just as soon as you stop trying to be a reporter.'" She cocked an eyebrow at me. "And he had that right, too."

"You stank, huh?"

"Like a senator's soul. Ned would've been the reporter in my family."

She took a deep breath, sat back finally. I felt like her grip had loosened on me. I stretched my neck out of my shirt collar. The collar was damp.

"Well, there's a lot of money in advertising," I said.

"Yes, there is. Yes, there is. And it's taken me twenty goddamned years to get up the courage to leave it and try this business again. And this time, I used every connection I had."

I gave her a nonchalant wave. "Okay," I croaked. I cleared my throat.

"Now," said Emma Walsh very quietly. "Now, let me tell you what you are going to do for me."

I blew out a stream of smoke. I waited for it.

She said, "If I tell you to learn the computer, John, you are going to learn the computer. If I tell you to get your feet off the desk, you are going to get them off, fast. You don't have to call me 'ma'am,' but when you talk to me out in that city room, you better *sound* like that's what you're calling me, you hear?"

I didn't say anything. I was plotting her destruction.

"And if we're in a staff meeting," Emma Walsh went on, "and I'm telling the assembled multitudes about the all-new perky, perky *Star*, you are not going to snicker, John. You are going to nod your head and rub your chin thoughtfully."

"Like this?"

"Not bad, but work on it. Work on it till you get it right." She sat straight. Her long hair framed her face. Her voice was even. Her eyes were calm. "Because if you will do that—if you will do all those things, John—then I will make this the newspaper of your dreams."

She paused long enough for me to say, "What?"

"You heard me. I will back you to the limit. To the wall and beyond. I will give you space if you need space. I will give you time if you need time. I will put the front page on ice for you. You understand?"

"Uh—no."

"Because while I play office politics—which I am very good at—and while I convince the People Up-stairs that we are going perky as a kitten in a ball of twine, I want you to blow this fucking town apart."

I may have stared at her. I probably did. My brain was racing to catch up with hers, but kept losing it in the stretch. I could only make another nonchalant gesture—a little turning of the hand this time—and keep trying to figure her angle.

And she said: "I want all those crooks of yours on the public payroll, John, my dear. I want the federal homeless aid that's being fed into the pockets of slumlords. I want all those wiseguys and good-fellows who're running the unions. And I want Dellacroce, not just indicted, but sent away. I want all those bastards, every one. And I want you to get them for me."

She fell silent, her gaze unwavering, her mouth turned up in a faint smile.

I placed my cigarette carefully at the corner of my lips. I pulled on it slowly, stalling for time.

"Man," I said then. "I'll bet your dog food sold like blazes."

"Top of the line, Johnny," she told me. She smiled wanly. "Now, how you gonna make me look good today?"

I rubbed my chin. I gazed into those gray eyes. I didn't know—I couldn't tell—what was going on behind them.

"You need an ally out there," I said.

"I do."

"You could use me that way. Give me nothing."

"I could."

"Then you might make it look like I've sold out."

"I might, that's true."

Still those eyes, those smart eyes of hers, didn't waver.

"If I find one perky word in any of my stories, I'll come after you with a blowtorch," I said.

"I'll be waiting. Now what've you got?"

I watched her, studied her. She still didn't give an inch, didn't reveal anything. I laughed. "All right. I've got a cop."

"I like that. Good. One cop?"

"Yes, but a very big one. And a very dirty one. A lieutenant named Tom Watts."

"A lieutenant, yeah, good."

"A few years back he was a captain named Tom

Watts, only then I found out he'd turned an entire
precinct into a drug operation."

"Son of a bitch."

"I wrote a bunch of stories about it, but I never
could nail him directly." I got to my feet and paced
up and down in front of Emma's desk. She watched
me, half-smiling, her eyes sparkling. "Watts didn't
much like being broken, though. So one day he
picked me up. On a pretense. For questioning. And
he beat the shit out of me."

"Oooh, bad move."

"I promised—I promised I'd have his badge for
that."

"Good. Good. And now..."

I stopped pacing. I leaned on her desk, looking
down at her. She looked up at me. I could see her
red sweater rise and fall with her breath.

"Are you dicking me around, lady?"

"You won't know until you try me, will you?"

"Fifteen years ago, Tom Watts helped some mob-
sters kill an informer. They buried him alive."

The half-smile vanished from her face. "Have you
got that solid?"

"I've got it awfully good. A deathbed confession
from a cop who was in on it. They'd admit it as
evidence in a court of law."

"If this is just a vendetta..."

"It's a vendetta, all right. He sucker-punched me."

"I want it solid, John. That's all I ask."

"Give me a day. It's an old case. No one will beat
us. Give me till tomorrow, tops."

"I want it solid," she said, "because if the mob

thought they could buy a cop, there must have been more than one. . . ."

"That's it. That's it." I smiled at her. "There'll be cops all over us."

Slowly, as she looked up at me, a flush rose into the managing editor's round cheeks. It was a nice color. It went with the sweater. She stood too. She held her hand out again. I took it. It was very warm. It was almost hot.

"There could be hell to pay," I told her.

"So I'll pay hell."

"By tonight, Watts'll know I'm after him."

"Let him know."

"The cops could go silent on us. The commissioner could call upstairs. He's friends with Bush."

"That's my job to think about. You let me do my job. You just be good to me, Johnny."

"Think perky," I said.

"Fuck perky," said Emma Walsh. "I want to make this a newspaper."

I went to the door. I felt a little rush of blood go through me.

"I'm gonna thank you for it," I said.

4

"How was she?" McKay was right where I'd left him. And Lansing was perched on the cabinet again.

"Don't you people have desks?" I asked.

"We were hoping to get your desk," said Lansing. "Now that you're going opera-side."

"Come on," said McKay. "How was she?"

"I don't know yet." I sat down in front of my typewriter. "She's attractive, anyway."

Lansing went grim. "What's that supposed to mean?"

"I don't know. Just..."

"Like, real attractive?" said McKay.

And Lancer said again: "What does that mean?"

"Yeah." I cleared my throat. "Yeah, I'd say real attractive, yeah."

"Oh, you know," said Lansing. "This is really... I mean... this is..."

"What?" I said. "What?"

"Well, here's an accomplished, educated, successful executive, and all you can think about are her legs."

"Who said anything about her legs?"

"How're her legs?" asked McKay.

"Good. Good legs."

"Jesus!" Lansing came off the cabinet.

"Hey," McKay said to her. "Just because we think she's attractive, doesn't mean we don't respect her as the boss." He turned to me. "Does she put out?"

I laughed. "Shut up."

"I'm serious," said Lansing. "It's not funny."

"She's serious," I told McKay. "It's not funny, she's serious."

Lansing frowned at me. "Anyway, I thought she was forty-something."

"Lansing, *I'm* forty-something."

"Oh, why is age always such a big issue with you?"

"'Bye," said McKay.

"Come back here, you bastard." But he was already gone.

"And she's married," Lansing told me. "To a very, very wealthy lawyer. They live in Westchester."

"So what?" I said. "So she's married. She's my boss. So what?"

"Oh—never mind!" She stalked off to her own desk.

"So she's married," I said to myself. "So what?" I started to look over my notes. "Shit," I said. "Shit, shit, shit." I took a sip from my coffee. It was stone cold. "Fran!" I screamed. "Get the fuck over here!"

I snatched up the phone. I dialed the U.S. Attorney's office. I couldn't get Ciccelli. I asked for Gerard. I got put on hold.

"What!" It was Fran.

I wedged the phone against my shoulder as I lit a cigarette. "Why are you in such a bad mood today?" I asked her.

"Because I'm trying to make a good impression, damn it!"

"So don't bring me cold coffee."

"Not on you. On *her*. And you keep yelling at me like that." Her eyes filled. "I don't mind usually."

"Okay, okay," I said. "*Please* get me some coffee. Or I'll kill you."

"You owe me twenty bucks." It was Gerard on the phone. "That Hershiser is unhittable. What a game. What a great game. You get to see it?"

"Uh, not, no . . ."

"Oh Jesus, Wells, what an incredible game. Anyway, what can I do for you?"

"I'm doing a series on gambling in the U.S. Attorney's office."

"Ha ha ha."

"Or, if you prefer, I need you to dig something up on a fifteen-year-old murder case."

Gerard said he'd get me what he could. I hung up.

Gershon, one of our photographers, wandered past.

"Wells," he whispered out of the side of his mouth. "It's perky. Pass it on." He went by.

"Hey," I called after him. "Perky's not . . . it's not so . . ."

I shook my head. I picked up the phone and called my best source on the cops, Lieutenant Fred Gottlieb.

"Hear the one about the dirty cop who helped bury a snitch alive?" I asked him.

"Eesh."

"Fifteen years ago. Guess who."

"I know who. Who doesn't know who?"

"It's around?"

"Off the record?"

"Not for attribution. You're a highly placed, badly dressed police source with a high forehead."

"Not for attribution, I've heard the story."

"Who were the mob guys?"

"Woof. Let me see. Marino was one."

"The same Marino you just found in the car trunk."

"The same one, only alive. And Tommy the Blond was another. That's all I can remember hearing."

"Thanks."

"Who's badly dressed?"

I hung up.

"We're going perky, Wells. Load for bear." It was Vicki. Rafferty was standing next to her.

I swiveled to them. "Hey. Grand Central's across the street, okay?"

Rafferty laid a hand on my shoulder. "I just want you to know, John, that we're all counting on you to risk your job standing up to her so that we can smile and fawn and degrade ourselves in front of her and then pretend to support you when her back is turned."

"Listen," I told him. "There are plenty of worse things than perky."

"Emphysema?"

"See, there's one right there."

Vicki lifted her head and shouted, "Hey, everybody. Wells has sold out."

There was a general "Awww" from around the room. I stood up. Fran brought my coffee.

"Just leave it here," I said.

I hurried through the maze and around the city desk. Pushed out the glass doors to the bank of elevators. Lansing leaned her head out the glass doors after me. She smiled maliciously.

"Guess you two can sit around being perky together."

The elevator opened. "I can be perky." I got in. The door closed. "I can be as perky as anyone."

I took the subway to Little Italy. I walked the winding, cramped, and smelly streets, between the crumbling walls of painted brick. On Kenmare, I went in the side door to a small garage. There was a man there named Marty Rapp. He was in his fifties now, but he had the frame of a linebacker. Arm muscles stretched his shirt open at his hairy chest. Leg muscles made his jeans tight. He had a sharp-featured, bullet-shaped head and a widow's peak you could open a letter with. He was in the bay, leaning against the trunk of an old Camaro, smoking a cigarette. A man in overalls crouched down next to him. He had the car's front door open and was working on its hinge with a screwdriver.

When I walked in off the street, Marty Rapp looked at me with marbly black eyes. He kept looking until I was standing directly in front of him.

"You're not here," he said then. "Go away."

"Let's go in back."

He shook his head, his pale lips parting. "What? Can I talk to you? No. Can I be seen with you? No. Go away, Wells."

"It's old stuff, Marty. Nothing hot."

"Nothing hot. You're hot. You're the whole reason Marino got whacked. Who is that? Is that me? No, it's you."

"I also pegged Mulroney for that arson charge," I said. "You'd have gone down for that. You owe me."

He looked at the grimy ceiling. Then he leaned toward me. Then he tapped me on the chest with his finger. "Wells. Mr. Dellacroce is still talking a whack on you. Is this a safe thing for us? You tell me."

"Tell Dellacroce I've written my obit naming him as the cause of death. He hits me, it runs. Now, come on, give me a break here, Marty. I need to know about E. J. McMahon."

"Fuck you."

"Was Marino in on that?"

"Fuck you."

"Tom Watts?"

"Fuck you."

"Okay," I said, "we'll do it this way. If Tom Watts was in on it, just say: 'Fuck you.'"

"Fuck you."

"Marino?"

"Fuck you."

"Tommy the Blond?"

Marty Rapp put a cigarette to his lips carefully. "This is a living person, Wells. Have some respect."

"Thanks, Marty."

"Fuck you."

I waved as I walked out through the door.

Next, I went to see Gerard. He gave me an office and let me go through the file. I got a couple of possible witness names, a couple of cops' names. After that, I went to Bagel Nosh and got a garlic with butter and a cup of coffee.

It was past two when I got back to the city room. I

started making phone calls again, trying to track down the witnesses. I actually caught up with one in Arizona, but she wasn't talking. "I didn't see nothing then," she said, "and I didn't see nothing now." She hung up on me.

After that, I called an attorney who used to be with the D.A.'s office. Then I started calling the cops.

That was the worst of it. The cops. I know for a fact that a lot of them would love to see Watts crucified, but they don't want to see an outsider like me drive the nails in. More than once that afternoon, the line went dead in my ear. When a cop did talk, the hostility crackled on the line like static. One old detective told me to take care of myself. He said it just before he hung up. He didn't sound very pleasant when he said it. I wasn't making any friends among New York's finest. All the same, I kept calling.

Around seven that evening, Emma Walsh came out of her office. She started walking around the city room. Hands behind her back. A proprietary look in her eye. She nodded at a couple of reporters. They nodded back and then buried their heads in their work. She wandered over toward me.

I was eating dinner and reading over some clips from the morgue. I was tilted back in my chair, my feet on the file cabinet. I was tearing into a corned beef on rye and dripping mustard on the folder that lay open on my lap. There hadn't been much in the paper fifteen years ago about E.J.'s disappearance. It seemed to have gotten lost in all the news about the Conti hit.

"How goes it?" Emma said. She glanced at my

feet. I dropped them to the floor. I tossed the folder onto my desk.

Emma sat on the file cabinet, while I swallowed some corned beef. "It's good," I said. "It's perky."

"Careful."

"Really. I've never felt so...so vibrant about a story before."

She almost laughed. Almost. "Never mind that. Have you got it?"

I wagged my head, ate some corned beef. "Yeah. Yeah, I think I've got it. A lot of cops have heard the story, so it's been around. One thug sort of gave me confirmation on the names. A lawyer who used to be with the D.A. is on record saying he suspected Watts at the time. I was going to run it by Rafferty, then call Watts for his no-comment. Then we can see where we stand."

"Okay." She stood up. "You know, if you had a computer terminal, you could just push a button for that morgue stuff."

I smiled at her thinly. "Yes, ma'am."

I called Watts at his precinct. The desk said the lieutenant wouldn't be in until tomorrow. His home number was unlisted, but I dug out my Rolodex and found him. I called him at home. A machine answered. Watts had gotten divorced after the drug scandal, I remembered. He lived alone. I left a message on the machine. I said it was urgent. Then I hung up and waited.

The phone did not ring. An hour later, I made the calls again. I got the same answers. The bulldog deadline came and went. I called again, struck out again.

I gathered with Rafferty and Emma at the city desk. Rafferty swiveled in his chair. I perched on the desk, smoking. Emma stood next to me.

"Do we need him?" she asked.

Rafferty's bullet head tilted to one side. "We ought to give him a chance to respond before we accuse him of murder. We don't want it to look like a vendetta."

"It is a vendetta," I told him.

"Well, I know that. But we don't want it to look like a vendetta. And if we wait for tomorrow, you can track him down man-to-man." He looked at me with his deadpan eyes. "If we leave it a day, do we get scooped?"

"No. Not a chance. D'Angelo went in for emergency radiation last night. He's not talking to anyone. Hell, he could be gone already." I called out across the room: "Oh, Fran, dear. Would you please dial up St. Vincent's and check on the condition of Frank D'Angelo? Thank you." I said to Emma: "She's great, that one. You gotta watch her."

Rafferty made a noise in his throat.

"What about Watts?" said Emma. "If we let him have an extra day, it may give him time to get at us."

I shook my head. "How? How can he get at us?"

Emma thought it over. She shrugged at Rafferty. Rafferty thought it over. He shrugged back at her.

"Okay?"

"Okay," she said.

"Okay, that's it. We hold it for tomorrow." Rafferty

turned a stone eye on me. "It's ten-thirty, Wells, go home. We'll let you know if he calls for the late edition."

Without thinking, I glanced at Emma. "He's the city editor," she said.

It had been a long time since Rafferty had heard those words. For the second time that day, he almost displayed an emotion. He almost looked perky.

It was cool and pleasant when I got outside. The air practically smelled clean. The evening rush had cleared away, and only the cabs swarmed around Grand Central. Their headlights shone in the clear spring darkness. The storefront lights all up and down Forty-second Street shone. So did the streetlamps hangdog under the stately office buildings. And the office buildings pressed black against the purple surface of the sky.

I was whistling my happy tune again as I crossed the street. And as I walked briskly in the shadow of the concrete terminal. Past the bums lined up at the charity van, waiting for doughnuts and coffee. Past their bent shoulders, unshaven faces, yellow eyes staring aimlessly through the mist from the manholes. Still whistling, I went into the terminal through the corner door.

I picked up a paper at the newsstand inside then hurried into the vast main arcade. Under the constellations arching across the ceiling above, the beggars sat against the wall, their pants legs rolled up to air their sores. The cops patrolled. I rushed past, thumbing through my paper, humming my tune.

I went down the stairs into the subway. Caught a

Six just as I came down onto the platform. It was crowded inside the rackety train. I found a seat next to a gaunt man in a billowing black coat. His mouth hung open. His eyes were glassy.

I tried to read the paper some more. I stared at the sports section. CLASSIC! the back-page headline read. But I couldn't pay attention to the story. I closed the paper in my lap. I slapped my fist into my palm. The gaunt man stared at me.

"Hot damn!" I whispered.

I had him. I had him dead to rights. That son of a bitch. I don't forget. I never forget. He sucker-punched me. Now I had him.

There are some people who say I work too much. Lansing, for instance. She's always saying that. She says I drown myself in my work as if it were booze. Trying to forget things. Trying to forget my wife, who left me twenty years ago. And my kid, who hanged herself seven years ago. Lansing says I work to avoid my personal life. She says I have no personal life.

But she's wrong. She's dead wrong.

This was personal.

I could still remember how it felt. Lying on the floor of the interrogation room. Watts towering over me. Watts's shoes in front of my face. Blood dribbling out of my nose, smearing my cheek. As if I were some kid who'd been knocked over by a bully. I told him. I told him then. I'd have his badge, I said. I said it with all the helpless rage of the moment. Meaning it, but not believing it.

"Your badge is mine, Tommy," I said. "Your fucking badge is mine."

And Watts—Watts, dreamy-eyed and cool—he pulled his foot back to kick my head in. If Gottlieb hadn't walked in just then, I'd be selling papers instead of writing them.

I got out of the subway at Eighty-sixth. I climbed up the stairway into the sound of horns, the rush of traffic. Up here, the street was still jumping. Young couples bopped by arm in arm. Movie marquees glittered. TVs glowed in store windows. I walked through it slowly, my hands in my pockets, my newspaper under my arm. I whistled a happy tune.

My five-story concrete building stands across from a movie house. There's a low-slung shopping mall on one side of it. New high-rises all around. I pushed into the foyer. Picked up my mail. Got into the tiny elevator. Leaned back against the wall as the doors closed.

I was more tired than I thought. I shut my eyes. I smiled to myself. Tom Watts, I thought. I had him.

When the door opened, I propelled myself into the hall. Down the hall to my door. I unlocked it, pushed against it with my shoulder.

I came into the familiar semidark. The lights from the street. The red glow of the movie marquee. The cracks on the wall.

I closed the door behind me. I reached for the light switch.

And someone looped a cord around my neck and pulled it taut.

5

I opened my mouth, gagging. The cord tightened. I saw white and purple starbursts explode in front of me. My lungs pounded. No air. My face got hot. The strangler leaned back, nearly pulling me off my feet. I felt my tongue forced out between my lips, my eyes straining out of their sockets.

I reached behind me. I heard myself make a soft, choking noise. My pulsebeat filled my head. I couldn't hear anything else. I touched the strangler's leg. The white starbursts were going out, one by one. Everything was going out. The apartment was spinning away from me, getting smaller, darker. My hand fluttered over the strangler's crotch. In the darkness, I saw the pinetops of the Maine forest. I saw them reaching into the thin blue of the winter sky. I had grown up in those woods. My breath made puffs of smoke as I gazed up at the trees. My breath...

I clenched my hand into a fist.

The strangler screamed. The cord loosened. I vaulted forward. The cord flew off me. I crashed against the wall. I clutched my throat. I retched. My knees buckled and I began sliding to the floor.

In the rosy light from the movie house, I saw the

shadow of the man who'd tried to kill me. He was doubled over, his arm across his midsection. His other hand had grabbed hold of a chair for support.

My knee touched the floor. I fought to draw a breath. My lungs dragged the air halfway in. I started coughing. Out of the corner of my eye, I saw the man begin to straighten.

"Bastard," I heard him whisper.

I clung to the wall, coughing hard. Smaller stars than before now sparkled in the dim room. Still on one knee, I hung my head, retching.

"Bastard," said the other man again.

I lifted my face to him. I saw him stumble away from the chair. He bent and picked something up from the floor. I saw him, silhouetted, stand. He drew the cord out between his two hands.

I tried to say something to him. "Please," I tried to say. I couldn't get it out. My windpipe felt as if it were closed off. My stomach felt like it was about to come up through it.

The man came toward me with the cord. He stood over me. I looked up at him, still trying to say "Please."

He looped the cord around my neck again. I came up off the floor and slugged him.

I didn't have much in me. My fist felt like cement, my arm felt like straw. But braced on one knee like that, I had my foot on the floor to give me some drive. I drove up with it, pistoning my fist as fast as I could. I meant to hit him in the face. Under the chin. Try to knock him out, knock him back, just knock him away long enough for me to get out of there.

Instead, I caught his throat. I felt my knuckles strike against the yielding flesh and cartilage. I heard a damp crack. I felt something buckle under the blow.

Then I was staggering after my follow-through. The cord slipped off my shoulder. The other man was reeling back, his arms pinwheeling. Just as I steadied myself, he went over. He hit a lampstand. It tumbled to the floor, lamp and all, and he went down with it.

I looked around me. I still couldn't breathe. I hardly knew where I was. My neck burned. My head throbbed. I couldn't think. I remembered the pine-tops of Maine.

Then I heard the man on the floor. I heard him making noises, terrible noises. I lumbered over to him.

He was rolling, tangled in the lamp's wire. Rolling this way and that, trapped between the toppled lampstand and the leg of a table. One of his hands flailed up in the air. With the other, he clutched his throat just like I'd clutched mine. He was making a steady gurgling noise. Other than that, he was eerily quiet.

"What . . . ?" I said hoarsely, still gasping for air.

He kicked his legs helplessly. He thrashed back and forth. He reached up toward me. He made that noise.

Dread clenched in me like a fist. I stumbled back to the wall. I hit the light switch. Now I could see him. He was a kid. A boy with short sandy hair. I'd never seen him before.

His body rolled wildly over the floor. His face was purple. His eyes were bulging. Spit dribbled down the side of his throat. His legs kept kicking. His hand clawed the air.

"Oh Jesus, Jesus," I heard myself say. My voice seemed to come from a great distance.

I tried to rush to him. But the atmosphere had turned to water. I could only swim in slow motion against the tide. I watched myself swim. Through the familiar apartment. Past the rickety wooden chairs from the thrift shop on Lexington. I wanted to scream my frustration and panic. The man was strangling while I struggled to him step after slow step.

I was still coughing as I knelt down next to him. I grabbed him. Pried his hand away from his throat. His mouth was open. His tongue was wagging. There was a weird depression where his Adam's apple should have been. I touched it desperately, tried to mold it back into shape.

"Oh Jesus, Jesus," I said.

The kid kept choking. The purple of his face deepened. He grabbed at me, grabbed my shoulder. His eyes were bright. They were staring at me. They were pleading.

"Oh Christ, oh wait!"

I pulled free of him, clawed my way to my feet. I went for the phone on the table by the window. Swam to it in slow, slow motion. Tripped over the lampstand as I swam. Fell past it. Got hold of the table's edge.

The man thrashed. The gurgling noise became a high steady whine.

I picked up the receiver, knocking the phone to the floor.

"God damn, damn it!" I screamed.

I went to my knees. My fingers found the phone. They were shaking. I forced them in the dial. I dialed 911. I heard the ringing of the other line.

"Please, please," I said. I wiped sweat from my face. I sat on the floor, the phone clutched to my ear. I stared at the man in front of me.

His thrashing slowed. The phone rang. He rolled onto his back. His hand clutched his throat again. I still could hear that high whine. I still couldn't think.

Then a woman's voice on the phone: "Emergency."

"Please..." I said. A hoarse whisper. The words slurred. "Please help me."

"What's the problem, sir? Can you tell me the problem?"

"I hit him. I... Please. I'm hurt. I can't..."

"You'll have to calm down, sir. Where are you? Can you tell me your location?"

"Location?" I put my hand to my forehead. My head kept throbbing. My pulse kept hammering.

The man lay on his back. His bulging eyes stared up at the ceiling. His chest heaved up and down.

"Sir?"

"I hit him in the throat..." I said. "Choking... Where am I..."

"Choking? On something?"

"I hit him."

"Is he breathing."

"He *can't* breathe!"

"Oh Jesus. You hit him?"

"Please..."

"We have to do something..."

"What?"

"He's not breathing at all?"

"Isn't this Emergency?"

"What? I don't... What?"

"For God's sake, lady! Help me here! I hit him! Oh Jesus Christ!"

The man's chest was not heaving anymore. As I sat there, staring at him, talking into the phone, I saw his hand fall away from his throat. It bounced once before it settled on the floor. His face had gone a strange, sickening shade of blue.

"Sir... Sir..." babbled the woman on the phone.

"No. Oh no. Now look at him," I said.

"We've got to do a tracheotomy."

"What?"

"Have you got a knife? Is he dying?"

"What do I do?"

"Is he dying right now?"

"Help me!"

"Oh Christ!"

"He's dead, he's dead."

"Oh Christ! Oh Jesus!"

"He's dead," I said again. My voice came from far away. "He's dead," I kept saying. "I killed him."

6

"You don't know who he was."

"I told you: he was a kid," I said. "He couldn't have been much more than twenty. How the hell do I know who he was? He was just some kid."

I was in an office now. An office at the precinct house. A dirty cube of a place. I was sitting in a torn-up swivel chair next to a gunmetal desk. The desk was buried under papers and styrofoam cups. The death-green carpet was burned by cigarettes. The fluorescent gave off a dingy light. The white venetian blinds had turned yellow decades ago.

"All right," said the lawyer. "I know you're upset." He had cleared a place for himself on the edge of the desk. He perched there, hovering over me.

"I'm not upset," I told him. "I'm fine."

"It is a difficult situation."

"These things happen. I'm fine."

He was a natty, slender man, about fifty. Dressed in a tweed suit, wearing a bow tie. His face was long, rectangular. He had coiffed silver hair, thick silver eyebrows that hovered low over his mild eyes. His expression was calm, almost sweet, almost beatific. I don't know why he made me think of an executioner.

"May I go on?" he asked very quietly, very gently. "I know it's hard, but I'm trying to help you. I'm just here to try and help." He was the lawyer the newspaper had sent. His name was Gerald Morgenstern.

Absently, my hand went up to my throat. There was no bandage on it. I could still feel the groove in the flesh, the mark of the cord. I swallowed hard, testing for the pain. It was still there. "All right," I said thickly. "All right. Go on."

"So..." Morgenstern leaned forward. A lovable professor drilling his student. "You didn't know him, and you didn't let him in."

"We went over this with the cops...Oh hell, all right. I didn't let him in."

"The door was locked."

"That's nothing. Anyone could pop it."

"The detective said there was no sign..."

"You could pop it with a bobby pin. I'm telling you. I've done it."

"Okay, okay."

He held up his two hands in a gesture of peace. I sneered and looked away from him, looked at the filthy blinds over the window. Then I looked away from them, too: they made me feel shut in, trapped.

"What time is it anyhow?"

Morgenstern glanced at his Timex. "A little after four."

"Christ."

"We'll be here awhile."

"Four in the morning."

"You want more coffee?"

"Christ, are they gonna charge me or what?"

Now he lifted his hands in a different gesture. "I don't know. They're talking with the ADA now. I pressed them to decide so you wouldn't have to..."

His voice trailed off. I glanced up into his gentle gaze and felt my stomach turn. So I wouldn't have to spend the night in the cage—that's what he was going to say.

I swallowed again, hard this time. "How's it look?"

"Oh, fine. Very good."

"I mean really."

Morgenstern pursed his lips. He looked down at his knee, at the hand resting on the tweed. He drummed his long slender fingers. I gazed at the top of his silver hair.

I gazed at him, but I didn't really see him. I saw the kid lying dead on the floor of my apartment. I saw him flung back in the posture of his agony, his back arched slightly, one knee slightly raised. His face was that awful shade of blue, and he was staring up at my ceiling with bulging eyes.

For a long time—it seemed like a long time—I'd sat with him. Sat against my table. Stared and stared at him. I was holding the phone in my lap, I remember. The operator's voice was still going. On and on. I could not make out the words. Just the sound of her voice, crazy with panic, crazier than me. It was the loudest sound in the room for a while, her voice, her panic. Before the sirens started, anyway. The sirens, their high wails. They came to me only dimly at first. Then, slowly, they got louder and louder. Small points of noise spreading over the other noises of the city, over the operator's voice. On the window-pane, the steady red stain of the movie marquee was washed away by the flashing red glare of the cruisers. I glanced up at it and realized that my mouth was hanging open. I closed my mouth. I wiped the drool off my chin with a sleeve. The operator was still talking. I hung up the phone.

The uniforms had been the first to arrive. Two patrolmen, one big and husky and yellow-haired, one small, Hispanic, slim. The big one knelt by the boy on the floor. He felt for a pulse on the boy's neck. The smaller one knelt down beside me, looked deep into my eyes. He said something. I don't remember what.

Soon, there were more patrolmen. And three men and a woman from EMS. One of the EMS guys also knelt by the boy and felt his pulse, just like the cop had. Then the EMS guy looked up at the woman with him and shook his head: No. I lowered my face when he did that. My lips were trembling.

After a while, another man from EMS, a black guy with the shadow of a mustache, came over to me. He knelt in front of me, leaned his face into mine. His breath smelled of pepperoni. He put his hand on my forehead and tilted my head back. He examined my neck for a few moments. He spoke to me, too. I don't remember what he said either.

The Crime Scene Unit showed up, and the M.E. But I didn't stay for that. Two of the uniforms took hold of my arms and helped me to my feet. Each one grasped me by an elbow. I stood between them and stared down at the dead boy.

The patrolmen led me to the door. As I went out, I

looked over my shoulder. The boy lay on the floor, his knee still raised, his back still arched, his eyes staring, bulging.

They took me out.

"John?"

I blinked. I was gazing at Morgenstern's face now. His lips were still pursed, his eyes still mild.

"Shall we go on?" he said again, very softly.

I shrugged. "I don't know. What's the point anymore?"

"I know you're upset."

"I'm not upset. Stop saying that."

"All right."

"He tried to kill me. I killed him first."

"Yes, I know. Of course."

"Why should I be upset?"

He smiled. I guess it was supposed to be reassuring. "You shouldn't be. You shouldn't be. You acted in self-defense. I'm sure the D.A.'s people will agree with that."

I sucked in another breath. "So what's taking them so long?"

Morgenstern wagged his silver head. "Well... that I.D., you know. That's pesky. Once they get an I.D. Then they'll know what's what." His voice just kept that tone. That soft, gentle, kind-to-the-condemned-man tone. Rhythmic like a lullaby, his silver eyebrows going up and down, keeping the slow time. "The important thing now is for you to try..."

He stopped. The door to the dingy little room had opened. A man came it. He looked at me a long time, hard. Then he shut the door behind him.

The man was in his forties, medium height, medium build. He was wearing a black suit with a thin, dark tie that may have once been in fashion. He had a trench coat draped over his arm.

Gerald Morgenstern stood, but the man didn't look at him. He kept his eyes trained on me, only on me. He looked at me as he stepped to the desk. He dumped his trench coat on top of the papers there. He stood with his hands in his pockets. He never took his eyes off me.

"I've just been put in charge of your case," he said.

Then he smiled. His eyes were lifeless.

"Son of a bitch," I said.

It was Tom Watts.

7

Morgenstern came toward him, his hand outstretched.

"Lieutenant Watts, I'm Gerald Morgenstern, Mr. Wells's attorney in this case."

Watts turned to him. He turned slowly, tearing his stare from me. Dreamily, he gazed at the lawyer's manicured hand. Then he turned and looked down at me again, smiling his dead smile.

Morgenstern raised his hand to fiddle with his bow tie.

I traded stares with Watts. He wasn't an ugly man, the lieutenant. He had wavy auburn hair, round cheeks, a pug nose, a jutting, cleft chin. He was handsome, in fact. Except for his eyes. Those mean green eyes: the malice shot from them like beams of light. It wasn't easy staring into them, into the heat of them. All the same, I managed for a while.

Then I shook my head and laughed. I thought I was going to be sick.

Watts spoke. He spoke very pleasantly. "It seems we have a bit of a problem," he said.

"Oh my." Morgenstern knit his eyebrows, looked concerned. "What would that be?"

"Well," said Watts—ever so pleasantly. "The deceased in this case has now been identified."

"Ah. Good," said Morgenstern.

"Yes," said Watts.

"And might we know his name?" God, they were pleasant.

"Yes," said Watts. "Yes, you might. His name was Thaddeus Reich. He was a young man from Massachusetts. Twenty-five years old. A graduate of Yale and the assistant administrator of a private shelter for the homeless here in the city."

For the first time, Morgenstern faltered. His face went blank. "Yale? Yale University?"

Watts kept those green rays aimed at me. He smiled. Pleasantly. "Yes. Yale. He graduated with honors."

"Hmph," said Morgenstern. He glanced down at me as if for an explanation. I felt the blood drain from my face.

Watts, his hands in his pants pockets, rocked back comfortably on his heels. "Mr. Reich had no criminal record of any kind. He had no black mark of any kind against him. His wife, she was extremely upset when she heard. Not to mention his parents. Woof. They had to sedate his mom." His smile broadened. I saw his teeth, gray in the dingy light. "And Celia Cooper, who runs the shelter where he works? 'What a loss,' is what she said. 'What a loss—we all loved him so much.' I think that's a direct quote. Just like what they have in the newspapers."

Morgenstern—*my* lawyer—he chuckled at this remark. He shook his silver head, bemused. "Well,

well, well," he said softly. "This does make things a little more difficult, I can see."

Lieutenant Tom Watts chuckled right back at him. "Yes. Yes, it certainly does."

I joined them. I chuckled softly, too. "Get this piece of garbage out of the room before I rip his fucking heart out," I said.

The gentle smile on Morgenstern's face stayed there, as if it had been painted on. His eyes went blank, though. "Uh . . ." he said after a second.

Tom Watts parted his lips. "Why, Mr. Wells! Are you threatening an officer of the law?"

I stood up. My chair tipped over. It fell to the green carpet with a muffled thud.

"How did you bribe your way onto this case, you scumbag?"

"John, John!" Morgenstern had recovered. He stepped to me quickly. He took hold of my arm. "Excuse us," he said to Watts.

I yanked free. I started forward, toward the lieutenant.

"John. John. This is the police, John," Morgenstern hissed.

"This? This is garbage," I said. "Get out of here, Watts. I want a real cop."

Watts shook his head sadly. "I'm very, very sorry you feel this way, Mr. Wells."

Morgenstern came after me again, his arm outstretched. "He's had a terrible shock," he said to the lieutenant. "He doesn't know what he's . . ."

I stood directly in front of Watts. Close up. The lieutenant didn't budge as I leaned in. There was my nose, an inch of open air, and then his nose—and our eyes staring across the distance.

"I've been looking all over for you, Tommy boy," I said.

He grinned. "Now you've found me."

"I wanted to ask you about E. J. McMahon."

"John," whispered Morgenstern. "John."

"Oh yeah?" Watts kept grinning. "What a coincidence. I had some questions I wanted to ask you, too."

"What did he look like just before the gravel covered him, Tommy?"

"John. John."

"How was it?" said Watts. "Watching Reich strangle on his own Adam's apple?"

"Did you laugh, Tom? Did you share a joke with the good-fellows?"

"Why didn't you help him?" said Watts. "Or were you having too much fun?"

"I hear you laughed, Tommy boy. You and your mob friends. I hear you yukked it up."

"John!" Morgenstern had me by the shoulders. He was pulling me back. I stumbled a step away from the lieutenant. Morgenstern slipped between us.

Watts said: "How'd you really get that mark on your neck, Wells?"

"John. Let's use our heads," the lawyer whispered harshly. "What are you saying here? We've got to use our heads."

"This guy's bad." I looked past him at Watts. "This guy's toxic. If he washed up on Coney Island, they'd close the beaches out to Oyster Bay."

Watts laughed. I strained against Morgenstern's hands.

"John, John, listen to me," he said. His throat worked under his bow tie. His earnest eyes tried to pull my stare from Watts. "John, this case is already in the hands of the district attorney. We can't afford to antagonize..."

Suddenly, I heard myself screaming into the attorney's priestly face. "I have him! Don't you understand! I have that prick on murder, he shouldn't be here. He knows that! He knows!"

Morgenstern let go of me. His hands dropped to his sides. His eyes were wide, his lips parted. He was shocked, I think.

Behind him, Tom Watts clucked. "Tsk tsk tsk." His green eyes glittered.

"I busted this gutterclot for drug dealing," I said. I was out of breath, my voice gravelly. "I had him licensing drug sales over his whole precinct. He's not getting away this time. I've got him, I've got him solid."

"Mr. Morgenstern," Watts said. "Talk some sense into your client. Please."

Morgenstern just kept standing there. Watts clucked again, shook his head.

Finally, my lawyer spoke to me—softly. "I don't think you understand..."

"I'm the reason he lost his captaincy, man."

"I don't think you understand," he said again. He tried to smile. "We can't afford this now. At this point. We can't afford to do this, John."

Gently, he came forward, moving me back, away

from Watts. I backed up until the venetian blinds folded with a crackle against my jacket. But I kept watching Watts. He perched himself on the edge of the desk, where Morgenstern had been. He lit a cigarette. He smiled over at me. He winked.

Now, Morgenstern ran his hand up through his silver hair. He took a deep breath. "John," he said. He let the breath out slowly. "John, John, John, John, John."

"You're through, Watts," I said over his shoulder at Watts. "Smile while you can, you asshole."

Watts waved, wiggling his fingers.

"John," said Morgenstern. His voice dropped to a mellifluous whisper. "John, don't you see? We want to keep the damage here down to a minimum. The D.A. will be taking the recommendation of the officer in charge of the case. If we can avoid charges here, we want to do that."

"You shit," I said to Watts.

"Then, if charges do come," said Morgenstern. "Well, then, it's a good thing he's here."

"You . . . What?" Breathing hard, I turned my attention to the man. Morgenstern smiled with kindly eyes. "A good thing," I said.

"It's a good thing," he repeated. "If it comes, if it should come to charges . . ."

"Don't you understand what he is, what he's doing?"

"No, no, listen to me, John."

"This prick is out to button me."

"Listen, listen, listen," he went on, his voice low. "Don't antagonize him."

"I'll fucking do more than—"

"Don't antagonize him, and if it comes down to actual charges, well, we can claim the police were unfair. You see?"

"What?"

"We'll get you an appeal on violated rights."

"An appeal?"

"If it comes to that," the angelic lawyer said. "If it comes down to that, I mean."

I stared at him. "This guy, this Reich, he tried to kill me. What appeal? What're you talking...?"

"John," Morgenstern said quietly. He cocked his head. He smiled with dewy sympathy. "Yale, John. Yale University."

I felt my mouth go dry. Dry and hot, like that. Like someone lit a match in there and burned all the spit away. Morgenstern, his hands soothing on my shoulders, peered at me, smiling with his soft lips. Tom Watts, perched on the desktop, watched us and grinned.

I ran my tongue across my lips. I felt my hands shaking. Fear made me hollow inside, weak.

"Get out," I croaked. "Get out of here."

"John."

"Get out of here," I shouted. "I want a new lawyer."

Watts stood up slowly, slowly shaking his head. "A new lawyer, a new cop. I dunno. Where's your sense of tradition, Wells? Old friends are golden."

"John," added Morgenstern reproachfully. "John."

I shoved him aside.

"John!"

I stepped into the middle of the room, confronting

Watts. I could feel the fear coursing through me, cold and hot at once.

"Am I charged with anything? Are you charging me with anything or not, you bastard?"

The lieutenant spread his arms, a gesture of innocence. "Me? Why, not a thing. Nary a blessed thing, at this point. The district attorney's office feels the evidence points to self-defense."

I took a deep breath. "So I can go. I can go, then."

"Oh, absolutely," said Watts. "We just respectfully ask that you remain available for questioning. Or, as they say in the movies: Don't leave town."

I nodded once. I started walking toward the door. Watts's hand shot out. Hit me, flat in the chest, holding me.

"But Wells..." he said.

"Get your fucking hand off me."

He smiled. He did not move his hand. "I just want you to know, Wells..."

"Get your hand off, Watts."

"...that I'll be working very closely with the district attorney's office as we continue the investigation."

"Off, Watts. I won't say it again."

"A man is dead, Wells. You killed him. Someone has to pay."

I brought my arm up, knocked his hand away. My whole body shivered like a plucked string.

Watts stopped smiling. His green gaze burned. He spoke very quietly, not pleasantly at all. "The last time you did that, you wound up getting blood all over my floor."

"You want to see what happens this time?"

He considered it. I could see it in his bright, narrowed eyes. I watched him, my throat tight, my hands clenched at my sides to stop their shaking.

In another second, though, he relaxed again. He smiled again. "You know," he said. "That's just your trouble, Wells. It's that temper of yours. You oughta watch that."

"Tell me something for the record, Tommy. What did happen to E. J. McMahon?"

"Nothing," he said, still smiling. "Nothing at all. Compared to what's gonna happen to you."

8

For a second, when I opened my eyes, it was all right. There was clean daylight coming in through the window. A cool breeze moving around the room. The distant sound of traffic and people. That sad smell spring has.

Then I remembered. It sank down on top of me like a shroud.

A man is dead. You killed him.

I rolled over onto my back and groaned.

Someone has to pay.

I opened my eyes. The clock by my bed said 10:15. It had been nearly six by the time I got home from the precinct house. Nearly seven by the time I'd fallen asleep. First there had been the phone. The press calling. The wire services, the radio, some idiot from the *Post*. For a while, I took the calls. Told them Morgenstern wouldn't let me talk. Told them to try Morgenstern themselves. After a while, though, the night, my sleeplessness—the whole thing—just sapped me. I lay back in the bed, my clothes still on, and fell asleep.

I was still wearing the clothes. I sat up and pulled at the collar. I pulled at the collar and felt the groove in my throat. I rubbed my hand over it, swallowed hard.

A man is dead. You killed him. Someone has to pay.

I got out of bed, changed my clothes. For a while, I managed not to look at the spot on the floor. At the tape outline that still marked the place where Thad Reich had lain, where he'd died, struggling for breath. But when I went into the kitchenette to make some coffee, I could *feel* it there, that spot. I could feel it no matter where I looked. Measuring the coffee into the percolator with my back to the living room. I could feel *him* there behind me, knee bent, back arched, eyes staring.

I went out to the Greek diner on the corner. Had a coffee and a couple of eggs.

I rode the subway to work. An uncrowded car. A mother with her baby on her knee. Two women students on their way to Hunter, clutching books, talking. A working guy in jeans and a sweatshirt, reading the sports section of the *Star*. I looked at each of them as the train jogged downtown. My hand rose to my collar, tugged it up over the mark. My gaze came to rest on the guy with the paper. He was traveling over the back pages slowly, chewing his lip a little. Looked like a decent guy. Pleasant lines on his big, heavy face. A nice guy. Tomorrow, the paper would carry it. A Yalie killed by a reporter. Might even be the front page. Then he would know.

A man is dead. You killed him.

It was good to come out of the subway into Grand

Central. Good to be moving in the vast space with the fast crowd. From there, I stepped outside through a door onto Vanderbilt. Crossed the street to the concrete tower that houses the *Star*.

When I pushed in through its glass doors, I felt the rhythm of the city room miss a beat. I heard the clicking of computer keyboards falter, then go on. I heard the murmur of conversation fade, then rise again. I felt eyes turning toward me—then turning away.

Someone has to pay.

Rafferty glanced up at me. The others around the table—editors and reporters both—watched him, waiting for him to speak.

"Okay, John?" he said.

"Yeah. Yeah." I walked over to him. Rested an elbow on the top of his computer terminal. I shook a cigarette out of the pack into my mouth. I didn't much feel like a cigarette. My throat hurt. I lit it anyway.

Rafferty tossed a gesture toward my neck. "Looks bad."

"Who's on it, Raff?"

"It's not your story, John."

"Yeah? You hear they've got Watts after me?"

"You oughta take the day off. Take two. They're small."

"Who's on it?" I said. I lifted my eyes a moment. Six other pairs of eyes sank down quickly.

I looked at Rafferty. He rubbed his nose. He blinked. He fiddled with some papers he was holding on his lap. "Wally Wilkinson," he said.

"Christ." Wally was a Cambridge holdover. A man who once volunteered to dress up as a dancing raisin and write about what it was like. "Who picked him?"

"Word from on high. They're afraid we'll look biased. They wanted a reporter who hates you."

"They're halfway home. He hates me, all right."

"Walsh got them to let us use McKay for your profile. He has about four column inches to prove you're a saint. We've got art of you sleeping with Mother Teresa."

"Oh yeah, from the Christmas party." I straightened. Dropped my cigarette in his wastebasket, hoped it went out. "All right, then. Where is he?"

"Who?"

"The dancing raisin."

"John." Rafferty's voice never changed its level. His mouth hardly opened. His expression never changed. "This isn't your story. Go home."

"What the hell does that mean?"

"The lawyers don't want you talking until the investigation's over."

"Yeah, but I can slip him a few things, some details. Besides, I gotta write up the Watts story. I got his no-comment last night. In spades."

Once again, Rafferty did his routine: blinked, studied his papers, rubbed his nose, the works. When he looked up, everyone at the city desk was watching him.

"John..."

"Wells!"

I turned around. Lansing was hurrying toward me

out of the maze, her long legs flashing from her short skirt, her long hair flying out behind her.

"Wells," she said again. She reached me, put her hand on my arm. "Are you all right?"

"Yeah, yeah, I'm fine."

"You must be so upset."

"I'm not upset. Why should I be upset?"

"Oh God, it's so awful."

"Yeah, well, it could've been a hell of a lot worse."

She shook her head at me. Those blue eyes of hers were wide and a little damp. "And I think it stinks what they're doing to you. We all think it stinks."

"What, you mean Watts?"

"I mean Bush. The People Upstairs, the way they're—"

Rafferty cleared his throat. Lansing stopped talking, glanced down at him. I glanced down at him too and I felt that gush of fear go through me again, the heat beneath my skin, the chill inside my belly.

"The way they're what?"

Lansing's lips twisted, her eyes flashed. "Rafferty . . ."

"John."

This time the call came from across the room, the other side of the maze. I looked up and saw Emma Walsh standing at the entrance of the hallway to manager's row. Now, all around me, the city room's rhythm dipped again, like the power from an overloaded line. The managing editor's soft, slightly southern voice reached me easily.

"Could I see you in my office for a moment, please."

I didn't look left or right as I went to her. I passed

by the cubicles without turning. I felt the eyes follow me, though. I heard the tapping at the terminals cease. And I heard that whisper in the back of my mind: *Someone has to pay.*

Emma Walsh stayed where she was as I came toward her. In her pleated green skirt, her snug green sweater, her brown hair spilling long down her back, she looked like a former prom queen waiting for her husband at the kitchen door. But when I reached her, I saw the gray eyes were grim, the red lips pressed tight.

"Come on in," she said. She said it gently, sympathetically.

I wiped my dry mouth and went past her into her office. I stood in the center of it, and looked out through the window at the edge of the Pan Am Building. I heard the door close as she came in. I turned to find her leaning against it, her hands behind her, her eyes on me.

"How are you feeling?"

"Perky," I said. I stuck a fresh cigarette in my mouth.

"John . . ."

"They killed the Watts piece, didn't they?"

"They didn't kill it . . . Christ!" she said suddenly. "You've been practically strangled, how can you smoke those . . ." I looked at her. She stopped. "They want to hold off on it. Until all this is over."

"You mean in twenty-five years to life?"

"When the investigation's over, they'll—"

But the anger flashed out of me. I shouted at her: "Watts is *on* the investigation, Walsh."

She came off the door at once, pumping her finger at me. "I'm your goddamned managing editor, Wells, don't you talk to me like that."

She halted midway toward me. I looked at her through a drag of smoke.

"You learn quick," I said.

The breath shuddered out of her. She ran her hand up through her hair.

"I'm sorry."

"You said you'd fight for me."

"I did. I will. Ach!" She threw her hands up, moved away from me. Moved behind her desk. But she didn't sit down. She stood there, her fist resting on the blotter.

"Mr. Bush feels," she said to the floor, "that the situation is tricky. Because of his . . . association with the commissioner, our relations with the cops have been very good. And he feels that would be jeopardized if we . . . seemed to be waging war with them. As in: You bust our reporter, we bust your lieutenant. That kind of thing."

She did not look up. She did not see me lift my cigarette to my lips. She did not see my hand trembling.

"Watts is *on* the fucking case." I said it softly this time.

"The cops won't admit that. They say Derringer's got it."

"Derringer? He's on short time. He hasn't got anything. Emma . . ." I reached a hand out toward her. I didn't care if she saw it shake or not. "I don't know what that guy was doing in my apartment. I don't know why he attacked me, what he wanted, but I . . ." I had to force the words out. "I killed him . . . in self-defense."

She lifted her head finally. She looked at me. "I know that. We all know that."

"And Watts is gonna try to nail me for it. He has to. He knows what I've got. It's him or me."

There was a pencil holder on her desk. An elegant gold cup. She reached out and toyed with the yellow pencils in it.

"Wells . . ."

"The commissioner called him, didn't he? Bush."

"John, I'm doing everything I can. I won't leave you to twist in the wind."

"That's what happened, though, isn't it? And maybe Bush sees a chance to dump me without my going to the competition."

She sighed. She toyed with the pencils. "The commissioner apparently feels you've had a grudge against Watts because he beat some drug rap a while back."

"So send someone else to interview D'Angelo."

"We can't."

"Why not?"

"Guess."

I threw my cigarette into her wastebasket. "Shit!"

"Services are tomorrow at St. Patrick's. Noon. Without him, we couldn't even slip it to another paper." She tapped a pencil against the inside of the cup. "But lookit. The lawyers are working full time . . ."

"Oh great. Can't anyone stop them?"

"Damn it!" The pencils flew in a yellow spray as

she knocked the holder over with a swipe of her small hand. She looked up at me and the flint was in her eyes again. "There's more at stake here than just your bloody Watts piece."

"Hey. You're telling me."

"I am telling you. You don't understand what I'm up against."

"That's your job, sister. You don't like your job? Go back and sell dog biscuits."

She leaned across her desk at me. Her cheeks were bright red. "He wants to suspend you."

"And as far as I'm concer... What? Who does? Bush?"

"He can cut you off completely. Without backing, without pay. Without even a lawyer."

"The hell he can. He cannot."

"Read the contract, John. You're under investigation for a felony. He can."

I stared at her. I knew I was doing it, but I couldn't stop myself. She might just as well have hit me. Without thinking, I even fell back a step. I even ran my hand up over my jaw.

"He wants to," said Emma Walsh. "And the way the cops feel about you now, they'd be on you like dogs."

For a long moment after that, I didn't speak. I couldn't. After the night, after watching that boy die, after answering the cops' questions, after going at it with Watts—to hear this now... Something just bottomed out in me, it felt like. My throat, already sore, felt tight. My head felt thick and muzzy. I stood, feeling the heat in my face, wiping at my face with my hand. I thought of that kid lying on my floor. I thought about his parents, his wife, the woman he worked for. . .

What a loss, is what she said, we all loved him so much.

. . . and somehow it all made sense to me suddenly. Watts being on the case. Bush dumping me. It seemed like it was what I'd expected, maybe what I deserved. I felt tired, too tired to fight it, now that it seemed so inevitable. I felt I had no choice but to just sit back and let it happen. Let it happen the way it had to, the way it should.

When Emma Walsh spoke, her voice was quiet again, gentle, sympathetic. "Just get out of here for now, okay?" she said. "Go to the movies. Go to the races. Go away. Go home. Let me work on this for you. Let me do what I can."

I looked up at her absently. "What?" I hadn't been listening.

"Go home," she said. "Get some sleep."

I nodded. I walked slowly to the door.

"John," she said to my back. "It was self-defense. Watts can't change that."

But a voice answered her silently: *A man is dead. Someone has to pay.*

It was a long walk back across the city room. The place seemed to have stopped cold now, gone silent. On the far side of the cubicles, the people at the city desk were watching me openly. Rafferty screwed up his face as I came on. Lansing stood beside him, her arms crossed, her eyes on the floor.

McKay came toward me out of a cubicle. He had a

sheet of paper in his hands. He walked along beside me. "How's this?" he said. "'Even before his discovery of penicillin, Wells's reputation as a journalist was secure . . .' Sings, doesn't it? And you should see the Mom Teresa shots. Wow."

I forced a smile at him. Slapped him on the shoulder. We'd reached the city desk.

"Wells . . ." said Lansing.

"I'll see you guys later," I said. And walked past them.

A few minutes later, I was standing on the corner of Vanderbilt and Forty-third, my hands in my pockets, my nose lifted to the spring breeze. The business suits were striding up and down the sidewalk. The sweatshirts were pushing dollies. The messenger bikes raced past. The rags sat in the sun against the wall. It was almost twelve. The day seemed to stretch out a long way before me. I shook my head, took a breath. I wandered away from the office, from the terminal. I went down Forty-third to Flanagan's.

The place was empty. The sports figures on the wall swung their bats and passed their balls and posed at the ready, waiting for the lunch crowd to come in and admire them. I sat at the long wooden bar. Michael was on duty. He was standing at the bar's far end, reading his paper. Nice kid, Michael. Tall, round-faced, sharp-eyed. From Dublin originally. Very friendly. Usually comes over with a big smile, a word on the day's news. Likes to hear the inside story and so on.

Today, when he noticed me, I saw him hesitate. He looked at the floor as he came over. When he raised his eyes, he was wearing a small, lopsided half-smile. He looked embarrassed.

"Michael," I said.

"Mr. Wells," he said. Then he stood silent, tense. He seemed to be waiting for something.

"A cup of coffee," I told him. "And turn on the noon news."

The television was hung high in one corner. He turned it on with a control under the bar. All he had to do was switch to the right channel and there it was. The face from my living-room floor. Thaddeus Reich. Only he'd been alive when they'd taken that picture. He'd been ready to graduate from college, it looked like. His light hair was wavy and gleaming. His eyes were wistful and bright. His smile was broad and eager. He gazed out of the television screen as if at the future. He seemed to like what he saw.

And then there was Molly Caldwell. Standing in front of my apartment building with a microphone in her hand.

I groaned. "Fucking Molly," I muttered. She never liked me.

She peered at the camera with her great big brown eyes. The breeze toyed with her short black hair.

". . . until last night, Thaddeus Reich's life was a success story. A story of hard work and dedication. And finally, of commitment—a commitment to ease the plight of the homeless."

"Oh, gimme a break, Mol," I said. But there was no spirit in it. I already knew what she would do. I expected it.

Michael glanced over at me, then back at the TV. He craned his neck to see the picture. He seemed transfixed.

There was another woman now on the screen up there. An older woman with gray hair falling free to her shoulders. Gretchen Reich, the caption said, Thad's mother. She was standing in the doorway of her house, as if the TV guys had tracked her there, coaxed her out. She looked disheveled, her hair windblown, her blouse wrinkled. She looked like she'd been crying.

"No, I . . . don't know why this would happen," she said faintly into the mikes thrust before her sagging face. "I can't . . . Nobody hated Thad. He cared so much for people. Nobody . . ."

She couldn't continue. They cut back to Molly.

"Reporter Wells has refused to comment on Reich's death," she said. "Police say the investigation is continuing. Bob?"

As they cut back to the anchorman, I laughed out loud. Helplessness squatted on my shoulder like a demon. I shook my head and laughed sourly. Then I stopped laughing.

Michael was staring at me. His mouth was open. His Irish eyes were wide and grim.

A man is dead. You killed him, those eyes said. *Someone has to pay.*

I wanted to answer him. I almost did. I almost said: *I had to do it. It was self-defense.*

But I didn't say it. There didn't seem to be much point. He was right, after all. A man *was* dead.

Someone did have to pay. The mind has its own rough justice.

So instead, I said: "Forget the coffee, Michael." I lit a cigarette. Forced the smoke down past my sore throat. "Make it a Scotch. Make it a double."

9

Then it was Saturday. Someone was shaking me. Back and forth, back and forth. My stomach heaved and dipped on acid waves. My head felt like a bowling ball with a bolt of lightning trapped in it.

"Wells! Goddamn it! Wells!"

Someone was screaming at me, too. Right in my face. I could feel the hot breath of it. The noise made my teeth ache. And there was a smell. A pretty, delicate smell like lilacs. It was making me sick.

"Stabus, fabus," I remarked.

But I kept getting shaken. I kept getting sick. And the screaming made that lightning bolt of pain flash and flash again.

I became aware that someone had stepped in dogshit and then scraped his shoe on my tongue.

"Damn it, Wells, wake up! You can't do this. You can't do this now, wake up!"

I stretched my forehead until my eyes were torn open. There was a blur. A bright blur, too bright. It sort of shivered around this way and that, and I could make out glints and colors, shifting in it, like in a kaleidoscope. And there were images in there, images of people, many people, who all looked exactly alike, who all went spinning around a white center. Then, for a moment, all the pictures, all the people, congealed into one.

Why, I thought, *there's Lansing. And she's yelling right into my face.*

"Damn you, damn you, damn you!" she yelled.

I peered at her stupidly. She looked very beautiful. That delicate porcelain oval of a face, framed with blond hair. Her high cheeks with the faint blush on them. Her blue eyes with their wide black centers. Those rich red lips. It seemed a shame to throw up on her.

I swung my arm wildly. It knocked her back out of the way. I tilted out of my easy chair, pitched forward onto my hands and knees, and vomited onto the floor. Then I collapsed headfirst into the vomit. I could feel it damp and pebbly on my cheek. I could smell it. I wanted to move. But I was so tired. So tired . . .

Then I was in the chair again, the tatty yellow easy chair in my bedroom. I felt something cool and damp on my forehead. I rolled my head toward it. Opened my eyes.

Why, there's Lansing again, I thought. *What a coincidence.*

She had pulled the ottoman up next to me. She sat on it, reaching over the chair arm to swab me with a wet cloth. She blurred again and went double as I looked at her. It was becoming a bad habit of hers.

Now, the room around her was tilting and swaying too. I closed my eyes to stop it. It stopped. My stomach tilted and swayed instead. I opened my eyes. I stared hard until the various images of Lansing put themselves back together into one. The one image was crying.

I reached up weakly, caught hold of her wrist. I held it close to my cheek. Lansing raised her free hand to her face, bowed into it, and cried.

"I didn't mean to kill him, Lance," I said.

She nodded into her palm. "I know that. Don't you think I know that? Everyone does."

"Watts . . ."

"Forget Watts. To hell with Watts."

"It was just so . . . bad," I said. ". . . when he died. Choking. Just a kid, Lancer."

She wiped her cheeks with her hand. She raised her eyes to me. "Don't do this."

"I couldn't help him. I wanted to. I wanted to." I looked away from her. And I saw the boy on the floor. Thrashing on the floor, grabbing at his throat. Making that sound, that quiet, breath-empty sound, in the quiet apartment. Probably what Olivia looked like, what my daughter looked like, sounded like when she hanged herself. I closed my eyes at the thought, but it didn't help. I could still see the image clearly.

I opened my eyes. There was Lansing. Her arm outstretched, letting me press her cool hand to my skin. Still, crying slightly, her lips parted.

"Stop looking at me like that, Lansing," I said.

She snuffled. She shook her head. She whispered: "I can't. I can't stop. I never could. I wish I could. But I can't."

So I let her do it another moment. I even looked

back awhile. I was beginning to feel sick again. My shirt felt damp and the smell of vomit was like a cloud all around me. The pain in my head was now a steady, rhythmic screek: a cat clawing at the window-pane, trying to get out.

I forced myself to let go of Lansing's hand. I forced myself to push out of the chair. I stood up, and stumbled to one side. Lansing jumped to her feet and caught me by the arm.

"I'm all righ'... All righ'..." I muttered.

I pulled away from her. Crying, she let my arm slide through her hands as I lumbered toward the bathroom. I peeled my shirt off as I went. I dropped it on the floor behind me.

In the can, I pissed and then hovered over the toilet awhile. I thought I might puke again. When I didn't, I moved to the sink. Started the water running. I cupped some in my hands and splashed it up over me. I lifted my gaze to the medicine-chest mirror.

The thing that stared out of the glass looked something like me, only decomposed. The crags in the thin cheeks seemed to have fallen in on themselves. Gray stubble covered the long chin. The flesh on the high forehead was gray, too, and so was the widow's peak which dangled limp and damp above it.

I turned away. Stripped the rest of my clothes off and stepped into the shower. I turned the water on hard. It pulsed out of the nozzle, steaming.

I stood under the steady blast, my head bent, the water pounding me. Fragments of two lost days flashed at me from far away, like glass shards in the gutter. Mostly it was the bars. Cocktail dives way downtown. Places where I wasn't known. Mostly, I caught flashes of the bars and my hand wrapped around a Scotch glass, the smoke of a cigarette stripping my throat, burning my nose.

But there was more. There were other flashes, after a while, as I stood there under the hot spray. There were the papers Friday. The heads on the tabloids. The metro lead in the *Times*. I remembered haunting the newsstands, waiting for them Thursday night. Carrying them back to the bars. Poring over them, my hand gripping the glass.

Those headlines—they were hard to take. But the stories weren't as bad as I thought they'd be. Only the *Post* came after me: REPORTER KILLS YALE MAN. With Matt Flamm pegging me the "*Star*'s so-called ace metropolitan reporter." So-called by him. But then, he owed me one for stealing his car that time.

The *Star* went easy, Wilkinson or no. And the *News* put Bronco Nagourney on it, an old friend. Both of them played up the mystery angle, the investigation still continuing, that stuff. *Newsday* did the same and front-paged the Libyans anyway. The *Times* did its usual just-the-facts routine, no jump page. Probably took them a while to find New York City on the map.

The TV wasn't so tough, either, once Molly went home for the day. No one wanted to crucify one of their own, if they could help it. Like the papers, they were poised, waiting for the scent of blood. If Watts got an indictment, they'd be on me like sharks on a wounded shark. I'd have done the same. No big deal.

But there were still the pictures. The pictures of Thad Reich, staring out at me, eager-eyed. A smart kid, working for the homeless. Good son, good husband, good citizen. And the picture of me—my I.D. photo—fuzzy and ragged and worn. Blood on his hands. Even I didn't like him.

And there was still that voice:

A man is dead. You killed him. Someone has to pay.

Only the booze could quiet that voice. So I drank. And that's all I remembered.

Now, I got out of the shower. Dried myself off, wrapped the towel around my middle. I brushed my teeth, rinsed, spat chunks of vomit into the sink. I started to shave—and cut a thick strip of flesh off just under the jawline. The plastic razor clattered in the sink as it fell from my trembling hand.

I braced my hands on the sink's edges. I bowed my head. My blood dripped down onto the white porcelain. It mingled with the droplets of water there, turning from red to pink. I stood and watched lines of it run down to the drain. I bit down hard on my lip.

Then, after a moment, I whispered: "Christ!"

"Wells." It was Lansing. She was just outside the door. "Wells, are you all right? We've got to talk."

I nodded. I couldn't answer.

"Wells?" she said.

"All right. I'm all right. I'll be right out."

There was a pause. "I'll... I'll make some coffee while you get dressed. Okay?" Another pause. "Wells?"

"I'll be right there, kid."

I heard her moving away. I looked up at the door, waited until I was sure she'd gone.

"I didn't mean to kill him, Lance," I said again.

I cleaned the blood from my jaw and pushed out of the bathroom. A tart mist of disinfectant floated in the bedroom air. Lansing had put the place to rights, more or less. Swiped up the vomit. Made the bed. She'd even laid a shirt and a pair of slacks out on the quilt for me. I shuffled over to them like an old man. I began the long, complex chore of stuffing myself into them.

The smell was better in the other room by the time I stumbled into it. Lansing was frying eggs in a panful of spattering butter. The pot on the coffeemaker was filled. The broiler door was open and I could see toast cooking on the middle rack.

I wandered to the kitchenette counter, leaned on it. Glanced over my shoulder at the floor. Lansing had taken up the police tape, the outline of Thad Reich. I turned to her, tried to say something.

She didn't listen. She dashed some coffee in a mug with the swift accuracy of a former counter-girl. Banged the mug down on the counter in front of me. Turned back to the stove. I leaned into the steam of it. My stomach did a barrel roll. I braved the nausea, and took a sip. Slowly, my guts eased in for a landing. The balloon between my ears began to deflate a little.

"Oh man," I said.

"Some drunk," said Lansing.

"The drunk was fine. The hangover stinks."

"You're lucky I got to you."

"Yeah, what are friends for if they can't shake you till you throw up?"

"It was for your own good. I've been trying to find you for days. I've been trying to wake you up for hours."

"Maybe I didn't want to be found. Maybe I didn't want to wake up."

"Too bad. I had to get the super to let me in." She spun around, slapped one of my best plastic dishes onto the counter. The eggs on it gawked at me. Lansing slid two slices of white toast next to them.

She handed me a fork. "Eat the eggs."

"I don't want any eggs."

"Eat the eggs or I will kill you, Wells."

"Yeah? How will I know I'm dead?"

"The pain will stop. Eat the eggs."

I clipped a wedge of white from a corner and put it on my tongue. It sat there. I drank some coffee, washed it down to my stomach. It sat there. I groaned. Tried it again.

Lansing leaned on the counter opposite me. Her blue eyes bore into me as I tipped the mug back, gasped out of it, set it down.

"Now, listen to me," she said. "You've got to stop torturing yourself."

"And change my whole way of life?"

"I'm serious. You haven't got the time for it. The cops are off the record saying it's beginning to look like murder. Gottlieb says Watts is onto something, he doesn't know what. He says it won't take much to force the D.A.'s hand. Once there's an indictment..."

"I know."

"It's catch-up ball."

"I said I know."

"You don't act like you know."

"Well, I know, all right?"

"Good," she said. "Because your self-pity is just meat for that bastard. Eat your eggs."

I toyed with my eggs some more while Lansing poured more coffee. I sawed off a bigger hunk this time and managed to swallow it without too much effort. Then I tossed the fork to the plate. I pinched the bridge of my nose, closed my eyes.

"Well, that's no good," said Lansing.

"It works for me," I said.

It was a second or two before I could look up again. When I did, I turned away from her, toward the window above my desk. Outside, the spring weather had turned sour. The sky over Eighty-sixth Street was gray. The window pane was streaked with a thin, steady rain. Judging by the light, it seemed to be midmorning.

"Okay. Give me the rest of this."

"It's bad, rotten. We're all for you on the floor, but the People Upstairs have more or less written you off. I don't know which of their emotions is involved—greed or fear—but every day they don't clear your name—every day they don't build a statue to you in Central Park—Bush comes closer to suspending you. The commissioner's on him and the cops are backing him. They don't much like Watts, but they don't want him tried in the media."

"Why not? We're a hell of a lot faster than Internal Affairs."

She smiled with one corner of her mouth. Straightened and turned to the cupboard for another mug. I turned from the window to watch her. She was wearing a yellow turtleneck sweater and tight light blue jeans. It was good to see her move in them. She talked without facing me.

"To her credit, Miss Dog Food of Madison Avenue has been standing up for you. So they tell me, anyway. The word is she's practically used up her honeymoon period fighting the suspension. In that perky way of hers that's apparently so endearing."

She slapped some coffee into a mug for herself, and another dose for me. She looked up and caught me studying her. She smiled again, then leaned back against the oven, hiding the smile behind her mug.

"At least you're still alive," she said.

"Yeah, I have it all over Thad Reich in that department."

She clunked the mug down on the stove behind her. "All right. That's enough," she said. "That's plenty. I don't know why, but that Ivy League punk tried to off you, darling. You want to sit around here and drink, or you want to find out what's going on?"

"I want to sit around here and drink. Damn it!" I slapped the counter with an open hand. The coffee sloshed out of my mug. The fork clattered on the plate. "I can't believe they won't run the Watts piece. I *had* him. I had that bastard dead to rights." I clenched my fist. "That gets me. That's what gets me. *Him* after *me*. Christ!"

"Well, that's how it is. You want to live with it or not?"

"I want to sit around and drink. I thought we covered that."

But Lansing was moving now. Striding out of the kitchenette into the living room. I watched her as she stepped right across the spot where young Thad had choked to death. She went to the desk by the window. Snatched her purse from the desktop. Snapped it open and yanked out one of her notebooks.

She flipped the thin book open as she paced out to the center of the room.

"Here's what there is so far," she said. "First of all, Thad Reich... Did you get this from the papers?"

"Probably, but let's do it sober."

"A Yale man."

"That I remember."

"From Somerville, Mass. Father a district sales head for National Foods. Mother a housewife and part-time nurse with two daughters." She glanced up at me. "They're decent people, it seems like. Racked up—well, the way you'd figure. You know, they're not too sophisticated. They don't seem... They can't understand..."

"Why the man who killed their son hasn't been busted for murder."

She looked at her notes again. "They won't talk to us, anyway. And now they're pretty much shut off from everyone, in mourning, all that. They gave a couple of interviews right at the start. Nothing much."

"Yeah, I saw one Molly Caldwell used."

"That bitch. She's in my book for this. I talked to Wallace in TV. Wait'll next year. Where was I?" The flush faded from her cheeks as she surveyed the page, lifted it, surveyed another.

I spotted a cigarette pack on the other side of the counter. Snagged one, poked it between my lips.

"Okay," Lansing said. "So he's a smart kid, apple of his mother's eye, no enemies, la la la . . . Okay. Goes to Yale. MBA. Out he comes and he heads to Wall Street. Did you finish the eggs?"

I cupped my hands around a match as it flared. "I thought he was Mr. Charity Worker. Where's Wall Street come in?"

She sighed. "Well, that's the thing. Two years ago, Reich comes to town, following what seems to be his destiny. In six months, he's one of the hot Young Turks at Bennett-Dreiser. In a year, he's washing the sores of lepers."

"Did they bury him?"

"What?"

"Reich. Did they have his funeral?"

"Yeah. Up in Massachusetts. Are you listening to me?"

"I was just wondering." I held the cigarette to my mouth with a trembling hand. "All right, so first he's a money man, then he's a saint. What happened?"

Lansing lifted a hand, let it fall to her hip. "A spokesman for B-D said something like, 'Thad was not cut out for the fast-paced life of today's financial market.'"

"He said that?"

"I know. It sounds so much like bullshit, but I can't find any dirt."

"SEC? Ciccelli?"

"Nothing. He didn't have time to get in trouble. He came, he saw, he fled."

"What's his wife say?"

"She won't talk. She was up in Mass. for the funeral, then came straight back. No comment anywhere."

"So he turns his back on a life of wealth to help the homeless, and he's clean. I'm fucked."

"Well, wait." Lansing flipped over a notebook page, scanned the book eagerly. She took two steps to the right, two to the left, two to the right again. I watched her, the shape of her moving in the sweater, in the jeans. I thought about her cleaning up the mess in the bedroom. "Okay," she said. "Celia Cooper."

"The woman who ran the shelter. Watts mentioned her. She loved Reich. 'What a loss.'"

"Right. And she goes along with the Bennett-Dreiser guy. She says basically Reich found the Wall Street life empty and—'spiritually unsatisfying,' she said—and started working for her to try to make sense of things."

"I killed Gandhi."

She stopped pacing, one leg out, one hip jutting. "Look. I figure there are two possibilities. One is that Reich was robbing your apartment and you surprised him. Now, given the facts that you have nothing and he wanted nothing, that seems pretty unlikely."

"What's the other possibility?"

"That there's some connection between you two."

"I never heard of him."

"No." She took a long stride until she stood beside me. I could smell her scent again. It did not make me sick anymore. "But you have heard of Cooper. The shelter she runs is the Cooper House."

"In River City. Yeah, sure. I've heard of it. So what?"

"So you covered it."

"Cooper House?"

There was a loose sheet clipped into her notebook. She pulled it out, handed it to me. I unfolded it, looked it over. It was a printout of a piece under my byline: BD OF EST GIVES SHELTER OKAY. A few column inches that had run in the metro section. I handed it back to her.

"That was five years ago, Lancer."

She stood over me, glaring down. "I tried to get a private interview with Celia Cooper. To ask her if there was anything about Reich that would help us. Know what she said? 'If John Wells wants to dish up dirt on that fine young man to save his hide, let him do it himself.'"

"But this board thing wasn't even my story. I picked it up for Stertz, I think, 'cause his wife was sick."

"If Watts sends you to prison for life," Lansing said, "I marry for money."

I laughed. The pain of it echoed up and down me. I ran my hand up through my hair.

"All right," I said. "All right. I'll check it out."

10

The rich of River City always look to the west. The collection of elegant brick towers on Manhattan's East Side hangs over one of the best river views in town. But in the twenties, when the complex was built, the East River was not as pleasant to look at as it is today. Where the United Nations Building now stands—its gleaming tower, its fluttering circle of flags, its shady park—there were only slaughterhouses, maybe a few breweries. Chester Daniels, the millionaire developer who erected the complex, built its apartments to face away from the water. The eyes of the wealthy would not see, their noses would not smell, the dirty business going on behind their backs.

Daniels arranged for the comforts of his tenants in other ways too. After clearing out the crumbling tenements that used to occupy the spot, he hoisted his little world on abutments over First Avenue. There, he laid out grassy parks, a playground, a golf course, a swimming pool, even a hotel for the River City folk to enjoy at leisure. Strolling on the bridge that crosses the broad, uncertain vista of Forty-second Street, you feel you're in another town. A higher town than the people down below.

Still, the River Cityans have suffered indignities like the rest of us. About twenty years ago, the area was bought out by Wilhelm Sturgeon, the hotel magnate, the one who looks like a toad. He wanted more rent, and that meant more towers. So the swimming pool and the golf course are gone. The playground and the parks were almost lost, too, but the residents fought back. As of this minute, they seem to have Sturgeon at bay.

But then there's the little matter of Cooper House. It's a wide old limestone structure, seven stories high, with plenty of ornate designs and dragons and pilasters carved into the front. It fits in well with the general ambience of the little city. But it sits on the corner of Forty-first Street and Second Avenue. On the border of River City, that is. It's not part of River City itself.

Cooper House has always belonged to the Cooper family, the once-mighty clan of nearby Murray Hill. Specifically, now, it is the sole inheritance of the black sheep of this family: Celia.

Black-sheep-wise, Celia hasn't exactly been a standout. She had her part in the student riots at the University of California at Berkeley in the sixties. She joined the Peace Corps and taught English to Ethiopians. And when she came back to New York, she got a degree in social work and was employed first by the Department of Human Services and then by a private clinic. Nothing too offensive. It just didn't put her sixteen million dollars in assets to very good use.

About seven years ago, not long after she inherited

the property on the border of River City, she announced that she would seek a zoning variance in order to turn the place into a shelter for the homeless. This didn't exactly please the River City people, on the one hand. On the other, being privileged, decent, and largely charitable citizens, they recognized the growing need. After a few public hearings, where they voiced their concerns, most of them decided to let Celia go about her business.

Not so Wilhelm Sturgeon. Privileged enough, he's never been caught out being decent or charitable. He was once heard to remark that, if he were mayor, the police would be ordered to lock arms in Battery Park and march north to the Harlem River, driving the homeless before them as they went.

Sturgeon did not attend the public hearings. He didn't have to. He knows how the city operates and, from all accounts, he operates pretty much the same way. He retains a law firm connected to the City Council president and a PR firm connected to the mayor. He distributes many thousands of dollars in campaign contributions to the borough presidents of Manhattan, Brooklyn, the Bronx, Staten Island, and Queens. So when it's time for a vote, he just sits back and awaits the final word from the Board of Estimate, which happens to be composed of the mayor, the City Council president, the city comptroller, and the five borough presidents.

All this is more or less legal, and also more or less certain to work. So it was a reasonably interesting story when the board turned around and approved the Cooper House plan. That gave Cooper the go-ahead to start providing services to the homeless on the very border of Sturgeon's land.

The few reporters covering the story did not have far to look for a reason. The comptroller, Howard Baumgarten, had lobbied hard in favor of the Cooper proposal. This was kind of odd because Baumgarten is a notorious party hack who's about as hard to buy as a pack of gum. But then, there did happen to be a federal investigation under way into an alleged kickback scheme he was running. And this community-minded action gave him the chance to appear before a stunned and bewildered media and utter the words: "I guess this proves we aren't all slaves to the dollar bill."

Yeah, we knew that—went the general reaction—but who the hell told him?

Anyway, Baumgarten won the day. Celia Cooper got her variance. The U.S. Attorney's office was all over the comptroller, looking for evidence of a money-for-jobs operation. But no indictment ever did come down.

Most of this story did not even make the papers. It was unprovable, for one thing. For another, it was too complicated. And for another, no one would have read it anyway. And for another, Stertz's wife was sick and I had a cold.

So I had to think long and hard to remember it all as I rode the subway downtown. I sat in a soggy, unsteady car, alone except for a black bum asleep in a corner under his slouch hat. I worked it all over, tried to get it straight in my head. It kept my thoughts off the jostling of the car, the noise of the wheels, the sloshing in my belly, the screaking pain in my head.

I got out at Grand Central and hit the air on Forty-second Street. A thin mist of rain was still falling. The spring hung heavy and damp all around.

I walked over to Second Avenue. The brick apartments of River City rose before me, floated above me, as I came. The skin on my face was chilly and my overcoat was dark with rain by the time I turned on Second and walked over to Forty-first. There, at the foot of the hill leading up to the River City complex, was Cooper House. Chiseled dragons and wisps on its limestone face. A castellated peak fading gray into the gray sky.

The front doors were dark brown wood laced with iron. They arched up to a peak like a castle's doors. They were closed, but unlocked, and I pushed in through them. Came into a spacious hall. Walls lined with bulletin boards and notices, children's drawings and public-service ads. The only traces of the foyer's former elegance were the immense chandelier hanging from its high ceiling and the tiled floor that reflected its light.

"The drop-in center's through the doors to your right."

I turned toward the voice. A woman leaned out of a doorway to my left. An attractive young black woman with a nice smile.

"There're no meals until six and we don't register for rooms until five."

"I'm looking for Celia Cooper," I told her.

"And your name is?"

"John . . ." I paused, then said it: "Wells."

Her smile vanished. Her large brown eyes seemed to go dark. Leaning in toward me, with her hands braced on the doorjamb like a visiting neighbor, she looked me up and down one long time. Not with anger or disgust. With sadness, it seemed like. I almost felt myself stoop under the weight of that glance.

Then the woman said quietly: "Just a moment. I'll see if she's in." And she turned and disappeared from the door.

I stood alone in the hall, under the chandelier. I lit a cigarette. I tapped my foot against the tiles. I wondered who dusted all those crystal prisms. I cleared my throat loudly against the silence. After a while I craned my neck, peeked in through the door that still remained open. I saw part of a front office with a desk just inside. Yellow walls. Another bulletin board. I could not see the woman. I studied my feet. I smoked.

"So what was it?"

I pivoted. Turned full around to face a man standing in the doorway behind me. He was a small guy. White, thin, maybe twenty, maybe less. He wore jeans and a white T-shirt, his sinewy arms bare. He had a sharp, heroic chin and a high brow. Blond hair that fell in a shock on his forehead. Thick, sensual lips curled in a sneer. Blue eyes narrowed in disgust.

My nerves were shot. The second I saw him—the

second I heard his voice—I felt sweat start under my hairline. I cursed it, tried to keep my voice steady.

"You talking to me, kid?"

He snorted, nodded. "Yeah. Yeah, I'm talking to you. Old man." He came forward a step, then another. There was an arrogant bounce in his walk. Chin leading, chest out. "I want to know what it was."

I took another drag of my cigarette, watching him come on through the wisp of smoke. He started to circle me. I turned slowly on my heel to follow him.

"Was it money?" he said. The bounce of his walk became more exaggerated. He got nearer as he circled. "Can't have been money. Thad never had much money on him." He grinned maliciously, almost dancing as he walked. "Was it sex? That it? He wouldn't give you what you wanted? Or maybe it was just fun. You like watching people die, maybe. What was it, man? Why'd you kill him? Huh?"

My heel squeaked as I turned and turned on it. He continued his circle, inching closer. Smiling that twisted smile.

And then he screamed: "What was it?"

The smile gone, the eyes flaring like torches, he darted at me. Pulled up only a foot away. He stuck his chin out at me, bared his teeth. His arms were out from his side, bent, ready. My throat tightened with rage as I felt his hot breath wash over me.

"Talk, you asshole. What did you do it for?"

"Back off me, kid. I've had a rough couple of days."

"Oh yeah? Oh yeah?" He smiled again. "You gonna

get mad? You gonna murder me too? I'd like to see that. I'd like to see you try."

I hissed through my teeth, kept silent, feeling the heat of his breath, the heat of his eyes.

Now he grinned. "You ain't doing nothing. You ain't doing nothing to me. You shit-faced coward. You kill a man like Thad. He's no fighter. When I did the streets, I had johns could've thrown you through a window *one* hand, they didn't fuck with me. You wanna fuck with me, killer?"

My hand flashed out before I could stop it. I grabbed him by the front of his shirt.

He stuck a stiletto under my upper lip. He grinned into my face.

"Oh, officer," he whispered. "He attacked me. It was self-defense."

I felt the cold metal against my gum. I felt the point pressing against the soft flesh. Felt the rage coming off me like waves. Heard my pulsebeat everywhere, the whole room throbbing with it.

Then a voice from behind me. A woman's voice. A weary voice:

"Knock it off, Mark. Jesus. Aren't things bad enough?"

11

The kid yanked the switchblade out of my mouth. A warm trickle of blood followed it. I spat it at him, our eyes locking.

Celia Cooper walked to us. Her flats whapped the tiled floor. She had her hand out.

"Give it here," she said.

He didn't even hesitate. He didn't even look from me to her. He just handed her the stiletto. Gingerly, she pressed the blade back into the case.

"Weapons are out," said Celia Cooper. "One more weapon and *you're* out."

He sneered at me. "Meet the man who killed Thad."

She didn't turn. "I'll deal with him," she told the kid. "What are you supposed to be doing right now?"

He bared his teeth. His arms tensed again, as if to strike. I braced for it. But he only answered: "I'm about to clean the windows in drop-in."

"All right. Go on, then."

He nodded—not at her, he was still glaring at me. But he turned without a protest. He walked across the hall with that bouncing swagger, and disappeared through the door.

Celia Cooper watched him go. Her chin was high, her gaze even. Only when the door closed behind him did she turn to me.

"We're all a little upset," she said coldly. "I'm sure you understand."

I stuck my tongue under my lip, tasted the fresh blood there. I dropped my cigarette on her floor and crushed it under my heel. "Yeah, sure," I said. "I understand."

For a moment, Celia Cooper stood silently, watching me. She studied me openly, gazing as if in a trance. Still angry, I gave the look back to her. She didn't turn away.

She was an impressive woman. Only medium height, and thin. In her baggy slacks and a sleeveless T-shirt, she even looked gangly, almost fragile. She was in her forties, and her short, curling black hair was turning gray, her round face was puffy and lined, the olive skin sagging. But all this—it only added to her aspect of command. Gave her a look of weary wisdom and durability. The firm, fixed gaze of her eyes and the upward tilt of her chin showed it too. She was a woman made to be in charge.

"You know," she said now—and she was still looking me over—"I'm trying very hard to forgive you, Mr. Wells. And I'm not doing a very good job of it."

I pointed at the stiletto she held in one hand. "You're doing a better job than Mark."

She glanced down at it, made a face. Slipped it into her pants pocket. "Mark's relationship with Thad was special . . ." And here she looked me in the eye. "Although we all loved him." She gestured toward

the door through which Mark had gone. "Why don't
you come look?"

I followed her across the hall, through the door.
We came into a large, open room with two windows
on the street and the dull gray day. There were more
bulletin boards on the walls here, more notices.
More pictures by children, and a few framed posters
of impressionistic fields and flowers. There were also
two big hand-printed signs on either side of me
which both read: "No Drugs or Alcohol. No Fighting. No Sleeping. No Hitting Children." And all
around, there were people.

About twenty of them, I'd say. Men and women,
boys and girls. They were settled on the tattered
chairs and sofas that had been arranged around the
room. Some of the kids were playing with trucks and
blocks on the frayed rugs strewn about the floor.
There was a woman changing a baby's diaper, and
another holding a sleeping baby on her lap. There
were a few women talking softly together while their
kids played nearby. A lot just sitting, staring. There
were two or three men, all of them sitting alone, one
of them, in an old armchair, catching a few winks by
hiding his face beneath a battered hat. Most of them
were black. Most of them had that look I've seen on
the faces of fire and flood victims: that deep, dazed
peace you get from a moment's warmth, a moment's
shelter.

On the far side of the room was the kid, Mark. He
was standing at the last window, pushing a squeegee
up and down over the glass. His arm moved mechan-
ically. He watched the sponge, deep in thought.

Celia Cooper came to a stop and looked at him. I stood beside her.

"Mark Herd, his name is," she said. She had a thin voice with a hard edge to it. There was nothing soft in the sound at all. "Six months ago, he was on the street, selling his body. To buy food and a roof—and drugs, too. I don't suppose you and I can imagine how degrading that feels, how inhuman. To be reduced to that."

He ought to try newspaper work, I started to say. But, seeing her, I swallowed the words—and a drop of blood with them.

"He was raped twice," Celia Cooper went on quietly. "Stabbed once. He's tested positive for the virus that causes AIDS." She turned, lifted her eyes to me. "He's seventeen years old. You'll probably outlive him."

"I wouldn't count on it."

She frowned at me, but her voice stayed level. "Last January, Thad Reich saw him on the street and offered to buy him a sandwich and a cup of coffee. It was Mark's job to go with men, so he did. They sat in a diner together at a table. They ate. They talked. Thad didn't preach. Thad never preached. He just talked about himself, about his life. He had come to New York to work on Wall Street, did you know that?"

"Yes."

"He talked about that to Mark. How it had hurt him, led him to drugs." She smiled fondly with one corner of her mouth. Shook her head. "He talked about the pressures of Wall Street to a common hustler. He felt there was a connection." She shrugged. "Apparently there was. Mark came to stay with us and he's been here ever since." We both turned to look at the kid moving the squeegee dreamily over the pane. "I suppose," said Celia Cooper, "Mark was in love with Thad. But, like I say, we all were, in one way or another. And what I'm having a very hard time dealing with right now is the fact..." She choked on it a little. When she faced me, I saw her eyes had gone damp. They were no less firm and direct, for all that. Just damp. "I'm having a hard time with the fact that you're here to find an excuse for killing him."

Across the room a baby let out a cry. I turned to see him lift up his arms to his mother, wriggling on her lap. Behind me, Celia Cooper said:

"I just told you a story about how Thad Reich saved a young man's life. And all you heard me say was that Thad used drugs. Isn't that true?"

I snorted. She was good, all right. It was true. When she'd mentioned that, I'd felt a small surge of hope that maybe the man I killed wasn't some kind of visiting angel. I met the hard gaze of those wise and harried eyes.

"I'm not looking for an excuse," I said, "just a reason. Thad Reich broke into my apartment and tried to strangle me."

"I don't believe that. And I don't think a jury will either."

"They won't. Unless I can find some sort of explanation."

"Some sort of dirt on the man you murdered, you

mean." The harshness of the words surprised me. For a second, I saw the depth of her rage. I saw her tremble with it. Saw just how much of her formidable strength she was using to fight it back. In another moment, she brought herself under control. "I'm sorry. Maybe that wasn't fair. All right." She took a breath. Went on in her brittle tone. "Thad used drugs. When he came here."

"A year ago?"

"Or so. He had come to River City to look at an apartment. For him and his wife." Now, as she spoke, she gazed off into one corner. A group of young women had gathered there. They were sitting on the tatty furniture, talking quietly sometimes, sometimes just staring, exhausted. Celia Cooper looked at them, but I don't think she saw them. Her expression had gone vague, a little wistful. "Thad hadn't been in New York very long. Only about a year, I think. But he was already making very good money—and he was already coming apart at the seams. He was taking cocaine, not enough yet to ruin him, but it had its hooks into him and he knew it." She huffed softly, a wry laugh. "Well, he looked at the apartment and started down the hill. And he came by here. We were having a drug-counseling session just then. It's part of our program. There was a sign outside advertising it. He stopped—and he dropped in." Again, there was that fond smile, the damp eyes. "I just remember that hopeful, eager, well-to-do, bright white face—like a great big moon—in the middle of all that dark and poverty-beaten homelessness. Obviously, I noticed him, and after the meeting I asked him into my office. We talked and—I guess he'd just been waiting to pour his heart out to somebody. He told me about how his life was... out of control, I think were the words he used. How he needed something, some meaning in his life. A month later, he was working here."

"And off drugs."

"Yes. He never used them again from that moment. I would have known."

I nodded. I believed her.

"I'm not sure how much of this you know already," she said.

"None."

"So you say. And I do want you to know it. I want you to understand what sort of man you... Thad was. For instance, I should tell you that his hiring was controversial, at first. Normally, aside from our professionals, we hire our clients. Like Laurie, whom you met in the hall. Or Mark. All administrative work, handiwork, cooking, security—it's done by people who came here at first for shelter. Workers are given meals and permanent beds and a small salary. There aren't many jobs and—well, you can imagine—they're coveted. A way off the streets, a place to live. There was some murmuring when I hired Thad—the rich boy, the outsider—but it ended within, I'd say, two weeks of his coming on. The way he treated people, the way he extended himself. You simply could not dislike him for long. He was just... irresistible."

She said it almost defiantly. I let out a long breath, put a cigarette in my mouth, lit it. I looked through

the flame and saw Mark Herd, across the room, washing the same window again and again. Celia Cooper
looked at me with something like sympathy.

"Is there anything else I can tell you, Mr. Wells?"

"I don't know."

"I've told you everything I've told the police, and
more than I told the media. I did it because I am so
angry at you I don't know what is right, what is just.
And that matters to me. I want to be sure you've had
every chance to . . . find your excuse, your reason,
whatever. I don't expect to be quoted in print. And if
you do write anything against Thad—I mean, if you
try him in the press to keep from being tried in the
courts yourself—well, you will hear from me, and so
will the public."

I only had to look in her eyes to know it was true.

"Now I'll show you out," she said.

And then something happened. Just a little thing,
but I noticed it.

Celia Cooper had pointed her hand to the door.
She was about to go on ahead of me. Before she did,
she glanced back at Herd and called to him: "Oh,
Mark. When you're done with that, would you please
go downstairs and rebag the compactor. It's past
time."

He nodded, glancing back at us—sparing a special
look for me. I caught it and returned it and, when I
did, I saw the man in the battered hat move.

He was the guy in the armchair, the one who had
been stealing some sleep. He shifted. Lifted his
hand. Tilted back his hat. He was a bullet-headed
black man with a mottled scar on one cheek, a flat

brutal nose, and dark eyes. Just then, those eyes were trained on Herd and filled with murderous hatred. His mouth twisted once, quickly. Then, slowly, he lowered the hat, folded his hands on his belly, pretended to sleep again.

I hesitated. I knew him. I'd seen him before, but I couldn't remember where.

Then Celia Cooper walked out of the room. I turned and followed her.

"I guess I haven't been much help to you," she said. We were standing at the door now. The building's sculpted facade vaulted, dark, into the gray above me.

"No," I said. "You haven't."

Then she was gazing at me again. She seemed to be leaning toward me. Her thin, hard voice came at me with sudden urgency. "I don't think anyone can help you," she said. "I think you know that. I think you know in your heart that you've done a terrible thing. And that nothing will help you but to pay the price."

She lifted her chin, certain.

I turned away from her.

12

I wanted a drink, more than anything. To kill the nausea, to stop the throbbing in my brain. And to stop the voice that now began to whisper again:

A man is dead. You killed him. Someone has to pay.

It was Watts's voice. And Bush's. And Celia Cooper's. But it was my voice, too, and it kept going on.

You know in your heart you've done a terrible thing and that nothing will help you but to pay the price.

It was true. I did know it. I knew it in my heart. I knew it on the surface of my knuckles where I still could feel the soft cartilage of Thad Reich's windpipe breaking. I knew it behind my eyes where I still could see him dying. I knew it in the black weight that sat at the center of me.

I knew it—and it was wrong.

There was a bar right down at the corner of Second. I paused in front of it after I came out of Cooper House. I looked in the window, saw my reflection there. What the hell, I thought. I don't have to go to work, anyway. I don't have to do anything. I can sit and drink until the voices stop, until the images fade, until the heaviness inside gets lighter. And until Watts gets what he needs for an indictment.

I looked away. The rain had stopped, but now the mist was blowing thick across the avenue, erasing the view to the south. I hailed a cab, got in.

"Downtown," I said.

We drove off into the mist.

Lansing had given me Thad Reich's address. I didn't know if his wife would be there, but I didn't want to call ahead to find out. I sat back in the cab, stared out the window at the passing scene, the vague, gray blur of buildings. I did not think.

The cab let me off at an apartment near Astor Place. A hunkering old monster of a building. Brownstone with medallions carved above the windows, caryatids holding up the cornice. The glass doors of its entrance were flanked by two huge columns chiseled with snaking reliefs.

Inside, in a broad lobby of inlaid marble, a doorman asked my name.

"John Wells," I said.

"Not the John Wells in the paper."

"No. Another John Wells. The one who's here to see Kathy Reich."

He called up and announced me. He held the phone to his ear and waited for a response. He waited a long time. I stood in front of him and watched him wait. Finally, he said, "Hello?" Then, after a pause, "No. He says it's another John Wells." I looked at the mural of clouds on the high ceiling. "Okay," said the doorman, "up he comes."

Up I went. To the seventh floor. A long, curving hall. Her door at the end...

It snapped open before I reached it.

"Great," she said. "Just great."

She stood in the entrance, one hand on her hip, the other holding the door. Her flat, sturdy frame was sleekly decked: a violet skirt, a purple sweater, a string of pearls. Her face was arch, her black hair pulled back severely. She watched me come from under dark eyebrows plucked to a V. Her jaws worked quickly at a stick of gum.

"So," she said. "I guess you heard I was free."

I came close enough to smell her perfume, then stopped. She kept talking:

"Kill my husband then ask for a date. I like that. It's so Richard III." She looked me over, nodding. "That's a king. From a play. By Shakespeare. Christ. Thad was murdered by a man who doesn't know who Shakespeare is. He'd roll over."

She spun away as I stood there, and went back into the apartment, leaving the door ajar. I took the last few steps and pushed into the place.

It was a large space. Sanded floors, standing lamps, brewer chairs. African art on the wall, a mask, a tapestry, a wreath of reeds. High, arching windows, gray with the sky. When I came in, Kathy Reich was at a low glass coffee table. She was jerking a cigarette from a pack there. She torched it furiously.

"Mrs. Reich..." I said.

"Mm..." She waved her match out, dropped it in an ashtray, blew smoke at me with her arm crossed under her breast. "Ms. Morris to you. Anyone who murders my husband uses my formal name. It's a rule of etiquette with me." She stopped mashing her gum long enough to bring her cigarette to her lips again.

"Mind if I smoke, too?"

"Hell, no. I hope you smoke a lot."

"Ms. Morris..." I took out a cigarette, lit it. "I didn't murder your husband."

"Boy, is he gonna he pissed when we dig him up."

"He attacked me."

"Now, that's an interesting thing." She pointed at me with her cigarette hand. "I heard you were saying that, and it's very interesting. My husband, Thad Reich, attacked you. Right?"

I pulled my collar down to show her the mark. "He tried to strangle me."

"Tried to strangle you. Right. One time, just after we got to this city, Thad and I were walking hand in hand down Fifth Avenue when a drunk came by us in the opposite direction, reached out, and squeezed my left tit. Here. Hard. Okay?" She held her hand over her breast to show me. "I said, 'Ow!' and Thad said, 'Oh, gee, that must have hurt. Are you all right?' I mean, I don't expect him to get himself killed, but he can shake his fist at the guy's back, for Christ's sake." She snapped her gum, puffed her cigarette, shook her head at me. "My husband tried to strangle you. Good. Was this before or after Tinkerbell kicked your ass?"

"Look, I just know it happened."

"Uh huh."

"Did he have any reason to be angry at me?"

"You were punching him in the throat, that might have annoyed him."

"Had he heard of me?"

"I doubt it."

"Did he read the *Star*?"

"Does anyone?"

"Was he afraid of something I might write?"

"You think he was an assassin for Literacy Volunteers?"

I took a drag of my cigarette. A long drag. Hers had burned down so she snapped up another and lit it off the first. I shifted from foot to foot, trying to work up the courage to start again. I felt like Holmes after round three with Tyson.

"I'm sorry to ask this, Mrs. . . . Ms. Morris."

She tapped her foot impatiently.

"But I understand your husband used drugs at one time and I . . ."

"This, I take it, you get from St. Celia of the Open Mouth." She nodded rapidly to herself. "Good. I like it. Great. Go on."

"Could he have needed money? Could he have been robbing me?"

She snorted. Stuck a leg out, rested it on a cocked heel. "Well, on the one hand, we weren't as rich as we were before he took the road to Damascus. On the other hand, you've never heard of the road to Damascus, have you, so the reference is wasted. The operative point is that I work for a living myself, a very good living, in fact. Which left Thad free to traipse bountifully among the dispossessed. And anyway, if you were going to rob someone, would it be you? I mean, for one thing, look at your suit." She shook her head at me. Turned and paced away from the windows, spun and paced toward the windows. She propped herself on the window seat and let her stockinged leg swing in and out. She chewed her gum at me slowly for a moment. She took a pull of smoke. It was hard to read her expression with the light from the sky behind her. Just as well.

"Listen," I said. "I'm sorry I came here."

"Yes, it was shitty of you, I must say."

"Why did you let me in?"

"Curiosity. Why did you come?"

"Desperation. I don't really know where else to go. I didn't know your husband. I don't know why he was in my apartment. I don't know why he attacked me. I figured if there was some connection between us, you'd be the one to know what it was."

She let out a short, sharp laugh. "Huh. That's what the cop said to me. Sleazy bastard, the cop. I'd actually like you better, if you hadn't murdered my husband. That's irony for you." She hopped back down off the window, walked rapidly back to the coffee table. She wanted another cigarette. She got it, lit it off her last. "Anyway, you've all come to the wrong place. You should have gone to see Thad's father. Now, there's a man you could get along with. He had a theory about the case that could have helped you out a lot. When we were at the cemetery, laying the box with his son in it into the ground, know what he said to me? Leaned right over while the minister was speaking and said, 'Knowing Thad, it was probably one of those fag things.'" Her eye-

brows went up again. She smiled archly. "Like that?
To his wife? At his funeral? A great man, Thad's
father. A Lincoln. The answer to the musical question: What if Willy Loman had gotten a promotion?
Sorry. Another play. After *Richard III*, before the
Mary Tyler Moore Show." She paced back and forth.
"What was so crazy is, Thad thought he wanted to be
just like him. For a while anyway. Not that he
wanted to drink too much and disparage everyone
who evinced any interest in anything besides money.
But that is why he got his MBA, and why he got that
Bennett-Dreiser job, too. He didn't like doing that
shit, he never liked it. But he was going to be a
big-time stockbroker. Mm hm, that'd make Dad proud.
Except the only thing that ever made that asshole
proud was fucking his chimpanzee of a mistress
without getting caught. All he ever said to Thad was,
'I guess people've gotta *buy* stocks, but why would
anyone want to *sell* them?' Thank you, once again,
Eric Reich. You virus." Back and forth she went,
faster and faster, her words coming faster too. "Anyone
could tell Thad wasn't cut out for that life but, hell,
who could say anything? I sure as hell couldn't. Then
I'm a ball-buster, right? I mean, as if Thad didn't
have enough worries in that department, he needs
me telling him he's not big and tough enough to
make it on Wall Street, that'd be perfect. I could've
told him. Hell, I could've told him he was getting
hooked on cocaine, too. But I'm not going to be his
mother, forget it. Thank God he found Celia to boss
him around, it's off my shoulders. I don't want any
part of that. They can all run off together and find

the meaning of life. Hey, some people need that. But I mean, I don't know why everyone couldn't just let him alone to be the way he was. Why does everyone have to be He-man all the time? I mean, *I* liked him fine. Hell, *I* loved him."

She stopped pacing, ended the jag. Bowed her forehead to her cigarette hand. For a second, I thought she was gathering her thoughts. Then I heard her sob.

I stepped toward her. "Ms. Morris..."

"Get the fuck out of here." She straightened, swiped angrily at her face with the heel of her palm. The mascara smeared across her cheek. "Are you having a good time? Just get the fuck out."

I stopped. I nodded. "I'm sorry," I said again. I walked to the door.

"Goddamn it," I heard her mutter as I stepped into the hall. "*Goddamn* it."

Then she said: "Oh!"

Then I heard her weeping.

13

The mist was still thick on the high towers of the
city. The little rain had begun again. All the color
seemed to be washed off the face of the buildings and
the air drooped like an old willow. I could see it in
the mirror behind the bar.

I was in a joint off St. Mark's Place. A weird little
spot with weird little artworks hanging everywhere.
Looked like crayon drawings shattered into bits, then
repasted together. There were only a few people at
the tables, young people mostly, dressed in black.
There was a guy with spiked blond hair behind the
bar. The mirror was behind him. I watched it. The
dismal city came back to me from its glass.

I watched it over my Scotch. Sipping the sting off
the top of the liquor, looking across its surface past
my own reflection. Now and then I saw a car wash
through the puddles on Second Avenue, leaving a
spray behind. Other than that, it was motionless,
colorless, gray.

I drank, forced the liquor down. My throat felt
thick. Must have been the injury from the extension
cord. Or the sound of Kathy Reich crying. One or

the other. I could still feel the cut of the wire. I could still hear the crying.

I set my glass on the bar and lit a cigarette. The booze was starting to boil in me. It felt good. It seemed to be washing away my hangover a bit more every minute. My stomach was easing up. The throbbing in my head was slowing down. Even my eyes were starting to focus. I reached for the glass. My hands were still shaking. You can't have everything.

I drank and looked into the mirror again. What would Lansing say if she saw me here? It hurt my ears even to wonder. But I couldn't think of anywhere else to go. There were no more leads to check out, no angles to figure. Thad's wife had loved him, his fellow workers had. He hadn't needed money or been in a jam. No motive for theft, none for murder. Maybe he'd taken drugs for a while. Maybe his wife hadn't liked his employer. Maybe his father was an overbearing drunk. But all that was nothing, just a life. There had to be some link between his life and mine or else...

A man is dead. You killed him. Someone ...

Oh, shut up, I thought.

I lifted the Scotch to my lips. I gazed into the mirror. Past my own reflection out at the gray avenue, the gray rain. Somewhere out there, Watts was working. Working hard, it sounded like. He'd already talked to Celia Cooper and Kathy Reich. Probably had a strong line on other friends, other angles. I smiled. He was probably doing more police work now than he had during all the rest of his career put together. Who could blame him? He had a real shot at me here. The D.A.'s office had let me go because the evidence supported my story. But if Watts could construct another story around the same evidence— or if he could construct new evidence—there'd be nothing to stop an indictment. That could mean jail right off, Rikers Island. Only the rich get bail for murder two, and if the paper suspended me, abandoned me, it could be a long mean time before I saw the light of day again. Months maybe. Maybe more than a year, maybe even...

When I set my drink on the bar this time, the sound of it made the kids at the tables turn. The Scotch washed over the glass's rim, spilled onto my hand, ran down. I wiped my dry lips with my palm. Stuffed my cigarette between them and drew on it hard, trying to steady myself.

"Another round?" the barkeep said.

"Yeah," I said hoarsely. "Yeah."

What difference does it make, Lancer? I thought. *There's nowhere else to go.*

The barkeep laid a fresh shot in front of me. I lifted it eagerly. I stared across it into the mirror.

And the man in the battered hat stared back.

He was standing on the far side of the avenue. Standing in the thin rain, staring at the bar, at me. It was the same guy I'd seen back at Cooper House. The one who'd shot that angry look at Mark Herd. And it was the same guy—in the jolt of seeing him I remembered—it was the same guy who'd been asleep on the subway I'd taken downtown.

I lowered my drink again. He was following me.

I spun around on my chair. The moment I did, he

shoved his hands in his pockets, bent his head, and started walking away.

I slapped some money on the bar. I grabbed my overcoat. I went out after him.

He was gone by the time I came out onto the sidewalk. I looked for him up and down the avenue. Bodegas, drugstores, newsstands. The zigzag of fire escapes on the face of brownstones. The dark of the rain. I clenched my teeth, my fists.

And there he was. A block away, moving fast. His head was still bent down under his hat, his hands were still shoved in the pockets of his worn suede coat. He glanced back at me once, then turned the corner into Ninth.

I stepped into the gutter, tried to cross Second. A sudden rush of cars slashed down on me along the wet street. I backed up onto the sidewalk, ran up toward the corner. I was breathless now, my lungs stinging.

Now, the traffic broke up a little. I tried again to dodge through. A cab hissed at me, its horn screamed. I saw its fender bear down, the rain spitting out from both front tires.

Then the cab was behind me and I was jumping up onto the far curb. I couldn't run anymore. It felt like dragging a truckload of cigarettes by a rope. I jogged the rest of the way up to Ninth and made the turn.

He was gone again. Nowhere in sight this time. I stood on the corner, scanning the street, the cool rain wetting my face, plastering my hair to me. I felt the hope draining away.

Come on, I thought. *Come on.*

But there was nothing. On one side of the street, to my left, a wall of old brownstones faded from me, their stoops receding side by side into the mist. To my right, there was some kind of church, with an asphalt yard on one side of it and a burned-out brownstone on the other. The man in the battered hat could have gone in anywhere.

But my guess was the abandoned building. I headed along the sidewalk toward it.

In the rain, against the darkening gray, the brownstone loomed blackly. A great skull, it looked like, the broken windows staring like empty eyes. The stoop was half-shattered. The door at the top of it opened into darkness. I started climbing the steps and met the sour smell of urine, the thick smell of rot, drifting down to me.

I stepped inside carefully. I was in the ruins of a foyer. A snake's nest of tangled wiring twisted out of the busted ceiling. The chipped walls were covered with unreadable graffiti. On the floor, in the rubble where the floor had been stripped away, there lay a kind of garden of glass vials. Some green, some red, some clear, most blackened somewhere by smoke. Large, dark roaches moved in and out of them. One vial tinkled as a water bug the size of my palm bumped into it.

A stairway of rich, heavy wood led up from me into nothing, into shadow. I stepped to it, vials rolling away from my feet, others crunching underneath them. I stepped onto the first rise. The whole structure wobbled. I stood still.

I peered up, into the dark. The stairway ended in the empty air. The top steps had fallen down. The last stair reached for the landing across a broad distance. I stepped back onto the floor.

There was a shuffling noise. I spun to it quickly. A rat was snouting the rubble at the side of the stairway. I gave a soft gag when I saw it. It was about the size of a football. When I turned to it, it paused. Looked back at me with faint interest. Its gelatinous belly shivered as it breathed. Its long tail lashed back and forth behind it.

It was standing guard before another doorway. The door into what had once been the ground apartment. Now it was just an opening into an empty room. I could see the space beyond. The vials there winked and sparked out of the white debris, catching the dull light from broken windows. I caught the whiff of decay again, stronger now. Slowly, I moved toward it.

The rat wheeled and faced me, crouched as I came.

I stopped. I stomped my foot on the floor, crushing a vial. The rat stared at me with red eyes.

"Go on," I said softly. "You're disgusting. Get out of here."

"Well, if you feel like that," he seemed to say. He turned away from me, started snuffing the base of the stairway again. Then, pressing close to it, he started moving toward the foyer. I pressed against the opposite wall, moved in the opposite direction, toward the apartment door. We passed each other, with mutual respect and consideration.

I went to the doorway. My hand on the jamb, I stepped through, into the room.

At first, in the pale light, I thought the place was empty. The air was undisturbed and thick with dust. Glass vials and glass from the broken windows gave off a lifeless glitter from the floor. Here and there, among the shards, I could make out the shapes of rats wobbling and sniffing at the bases of the walls. On the walls' surfaces, black spots crawled calmly, more roaches, more water bugs. Other than that, nothing seemed to stir. It was a long moment before I saw the people.

They were sitting right there in the open. Against the walls, most of them. Some squatting further out toward the center of the room. Their faces were dark, but in the gray light they almost seemed to fade into the chipping walls, the rubble-covered floor. They were so still. Only now and then did one of them shift. And then there would be a little peak of pale fire from the hand. The quick hiss of in-taken breath. Eyes closing. And the long exhalation.

I let the jamb go, came into the room a few more steps. I scanned the faces, looking for the man in the slouch hat.

There was a sudden movement from the window. I turned. A woman climbed in easily from the back lot outside. Another man got up and moved to the window to leave. I stood watching them.

And a blow from behind drove me to my knees.

14

Glass vials shattered under my knees as I dropped to the floor. I let out a scream of pain and was hit again. I went all the way down, rolling to the side. My arms thrashed wildly to fend off another blow.

But it didn't come. Instead, I rolled over, came up on one leg. Saw the man in the battered hat running out of the room.

"Hey," I heard someone say quietly. "Shit."

I got up, tried to sprint after him. My knee buckled beneath me. I tumbled forward, grabbed hold of the jamb.

The man in the battered hat was racing across the foyer. Making for the rectangle of light that led to the street. He'd have gotten away easily if he'd made it out.

But he didn't. He slipped on a vial, tumbled to one side. Before he went down, he caught hold of a rotting banister newel. He began to drag himself upright.

I leapt at him. Pushing off the jamb, I practically fell forward, reaching out to grab him. My hands slid down the back of his jacket. I crashed to the floor. He started running. But I got him, caught hold of his ankle.

The man pitched forward with a shout, his hat

rolling off him. He slapped facedown onto the floor. I heard the glass crunch under him.

He twisted, kicked. His boot crashed into my collarbone. I lost my grip on him, rolled away.

I pushed to my feet. My right knee stung, burned. I fell back against the wall. I leaned there, panting. I watched the black man. He was reaching up, grabbing at the side of the stairs. I wanted to stop him. I couldn't. I was finished. A curse rasped out of me.

The black man got to his feet, but he didn't run. He leaned against the stair, breathing hard, pawing his face. He was hurt. The glass had cut him. Right where his scar had been, there was freshly torn skin, dark blood running. He wiped at it, looked at his hand. There were glass shards on the palm.

"Shhhhit," he said.

He looked up at me angrily, the wide fighter's nose flaring. I was bent over now, my hands on my knees, my eyes turned up to watch him as I tried to catch my breath.

With his other hand, he took a switchblade out of his pocket. Still staring at me, he snapped it open.

I waved my hand back and forth at him.

"Don't. Don't. I can't... I'm too... Don't."

He glanced at the blood and glass on his palm again. "Shit," he said. "You really hurt me. Fuck." He shook his head, disgusted. With a quick, angry motion, he wiped his hand on his filthy green pants. He folded up the knife and put it away. Leaning back against the stairs, he coughed a few times. He shook his head. "Shit," he said for the third time. "Shoulda thought about that mirror behind the bar."

"Who ... who are you?"

"Shit, look at you. You way out of shape. Look at you breathe, Jack."

I was trying to straighten up. My breath was whistling in my throat.

"You must smoke cigarettes."

I managed to nod.

"Good. Gimme one."

I tried to laugh, but coughed instead. Hacking hard, I reached into my pocket, brought out my pack, offered it.

The black man laughed as I handed him the matches. "*Look* at you! Shit. You'd die at hoops. You'd be dead."

He handed the pack back. I took a smoke for myself, wheezing. I shook my head. "I'd turn off the TV before that happened."

He laughed again. "You gonna smoke that? Shit. I thought I was bad."

I spit some phlegm on the floor and lit up.

"Shit," he said.

It was a while before I could stop coughing. When I did, I said, "So? Who are you?"

He leaned back against the stairs, smoking, his hand over his mouth, his thumb nudging the cut on his cheek. He stretched his feet out and vials tinkled as he kicked them away. He was a younger man than I'd thought at first. When he switched off the evil glare, he didn't look more than thirty

"I'm called Sam Scar," he said.

"Why are you following me?"

"I wanna find out whose side you on."

"Mine. Ask me a tough one."

"I gotta be sure. 'Cause I tried talking to that cop. He told me to shut up. Said I'd get in trouble."

"Watts?"

"Yeah, that's him. Watts. Told me to keep my black mouth to myself. Grabbed my arm. Shit. I'm on probation, man. I don't need no trouble with no cops."

"Well, then we're all right," I said. "Whatever side Watts is on, I'm on the other."

"Yeah, I was beginning to catch on to that."

I heard sounds from the nearby room. A loud exhalation. A vial dropping.

I coughed again. Straightened some more, braced against the wall. "Could we get out of here?"

But the black man chuckled. He didn't move. "Hell, no, man. I like it here. It's safe. The cops don't come in here, otherwise they might have to arrest somebody. Anyway, there's nothing dangerous about it. Just a way station case you can't make it to Third Street. Like what Celia call a drop-in center. Just drop in the window." He laughed.

"This your kind of place?"

"Me? Shit. Not me. Not anymore. Not this week anyway. Celia Cooper done showed me the way, brother."

"You work at Cooper House."

"That's right. Least I did."

"Herd replaced you?"

"Who said that?" His glance had gone dark again.

"I saw you looking at him when Miss Cooper asked him to do a job. Looking at him kind of the way you're looking at me now. She said the jobs were coveted..." I shrugged.

The black man relaxed. He flashed a broad grin, stuck the cigarette in it. He laughed. "That's smart. Shit. I like that. Wo, watch out."

He pointed to the wall I was leaning on and I turned to see a roach feeling for my shoulder. I came away from it.

He said: "So you so smart, how come you iced Thad Reich?"

"That's what I'd like to know."

His smile vanished. He stepped toward me. Glass ground under his feet. He cocked his eyebrow at me, pointed at my chest. "Well, Mark Herd ain't replaced me yet, but something's going on, I know that. It's been strange at Cooper House ever since Mikki Snow left."

"Mikki Snow."

"She's the bookkeeper. Used to be. One of us. From North Carolina, I think, I don't remember. Came here to go to school, got homeless. Celia took her in, she got to be the bookkeeper 'cause she's so smart."

"When was that?"

"I don't know. A year. She was there when I came."

"Now she's gone."

"Four or five days ago. Didn't even say a word. Celia says she just took off on her. She was kind of put out about it, too. Not like Mikki Snow to do that, she said. It wasn't, either."

He dropped his cigarette. It glowed among the

glass, then went out. He bent over and scooped his hat off the floor. He held it in one hand, swiped the dust off it with the other.

"What's that got to do with me?" I asked him.

He stopped swiping. Glanced at me coolly. "Has to do with *me*, Jack. See, before Mikki left, I was, like, what you call the handyman around Cooper House. I fix things. The stove, the boiler. Compactor. I did all that shit. I'm good at it. Now, I'm heading downstairs to take a look at the boiler and I hear Celia say, 'Never mind that, Sam. Mark take care of that.' Shit. Mark know about as much about a boiler as he does about pussy. Which is none. He used to work in the kitchen with the cook." He put his hat on his head again, flicked a finger over the drying blood on his cheek. "Now, she still let me do the job on the ovens I was doing, but that's not gonna take more than another day or so no matter how it stretches. When that done . . . I don't know. I don't want to lose this job, Jack. I lose this job, I'm back on the street again. Which is exactly where I don't want to be at. See?"

"No." I dropped the last of my cigarette. A rat— that same huge rat—turned to eye it curiously from the corner near the front door. "I still don't see what this has to do with Thad Reich."

He lifted a hand. "Maybe nothing. All I'm saying: it's a lot of shit at once, that's all. See, Celia Cooper— don't get me wrong—she a nice lady, but . . . she's white. She's white *and* rich, see? Now, it's not that she's racial or anything like that. Okay? But she just be . . . *trusting* her own kind a little bit more when it comes to it. You follow what I say here?"

"Yeah, I follow."

"Her and Thad and Mark, they be like . . ." He held up three fingers close together. "Thick, you know? The others, me and Mikki, Laurie, all the others, you know—don't get me wrong, we're treated fine, we just . . . the folks, see? The other folks. Trouble comes, they close ranks together, we have to wait, find out what's going down. See? Now, all of a sudden, Mikki's gone, Mark's doing my job, and Thad Reich—who got about as much fight in him as, like, a flower—he turns up dead in your apartment and when I tell this to the cop he tells me to shut my black mouth or I get in shit. Now, I'm gonna be out on my ass in a minute, so I got to tell someone. And you looking at doing time, Jack, so you gotta listen to someone. I just wanna make sure this doesn't get back to Watts or Celia before I come ahead and tell you. See?"

The rat by the door was snuffing at the wall again, waddling in my direction. The smell of the place— the piss, the death—it seemed to be crowding in around me, clogging my nostrils and lungs. The little flicks of the torches from within, the desperate sucking of air, the ecstatic release of breath—it haunted the dark like phantoms, floating and curling through the shadows at the top of the stairs.

For all that, though, I began to feel a slight shifting inside me, a weight rolling over. A few minutes ago, I'd been up against a dead end. Now I had something. Not much, but a direction, a way to go. I offered Sam Scar another cigarette. He took it grate-fully. For a few seconds, we smoked together, with-out speaking.

"This Mikki Snow, you have no idea where she went?"

"Uh uh. One morning, I come down, she's gone."

"One morning when?"

"Wednesday. Same day you..."

"Killed Thad Reich, yeah. And when did you see her last?"

"Every day before that. She was in the back office and that's where the stairs to the cellar is. I had to go by her all the time to get down to the boiler room or the compactor room or whatever."

"So you saw her Tuesday?"

"Yeah."

"And you said?"

"Just hello. How you doin'? Shit like that. Last time I really had the chance to talk to her was..." Hat in hand, he scratched his head, looked up at the ceiling. "Well, I guess the day before that we chatted a little. She wanted to know if I ever heard of some guy."

"What guy? You remember his name?"

"Yeah. Yeah. What was it? Howard. Howard something..."

I let a lungful of smoke out in a small stream. I was almost afraid to ask. "Baumgarten?"

"That's it."

"Howard Baumgarten."

"Yeah."

"The city comptroller."

15

The dark came down slowly, the way it does in spring. The air turned a rich blue, shade by shade. I rode a cab uptown, up Park, through the dusk. I watched as the budding branches of the sidewalk trees sank back into silhouette. I watched the skyline lights to the north rise slowly out of the background of the evening.

It was hard to sit there, to sit still, with my mind working it over. Howard Baumgarten. The city comptroller. The man who won Cooper House its approval from a bought-off board. It might be nothing. It probably was. A shelter like Cooper House would have to have some city grants, connections with other institutions, other agencies. Baumgarten's office was sure to have a hand in it. Mikki Snow was probably just filling out some form or other or making a phone call when she spoke to Sam Scar.

It was probably nothing, but it was everything I had. Everything but the whispers running on and on in my head. So I couldn't let it go, couldn't stop working it as the cab headed northward. My one connection with Thad Reich's life. The Board of

Estimate story I'd picked up for Stertz. I kept turning it over and over, looking for a way in.

The cab moved quickly in the light Saturday traffic. The massive front of Grand Central came closer, its chiseled Mercury spread his arms at me from above. I glanced up through the windshield to the west, toward the *Star*. It would be quiet there now unless a jet had crashed on the Garden or something. Ray Marshall, the weekend guy, would be at the desk. That meant there would be wastepaper basketball contests and a box of Dunkin Donuts by the coffeemaker. There'd be a lot of wire copy to rewrite and blotter stories to track down. Maybe, once the Saturday-night drinking started, there'd be a decent murder or two. If not, Ray would turn up the sound on one of the TV monitors and let fly with a running commentary on the latest episode of the latest cop show. Once I wandered in there and caught them all dancing to some FM rock. Maybe they'd be doing that tonight.

For a second or two, I thought of telling the cabbie to go on to Forty-second. Maybe I could drop in, I thought. Read the wires. Find out the latest from upstairs. Then I thought of the way they'd look at me, the things they'd say when I came in. By then, anyway, the cab was heading around the terminal.

And I started going at it again. Howard Baumgarten. The Board of Estimate. Mikki Snow—where was she? Somehow, I would have to try to track her down.

When I got out of the cab in front of my building, I stood on the sidewalk a second. I looked up at the windows of my apartment. They reflected the neon

of the street back to me. I thought of spending the
night in there. With the TV and the cracks on the
wall, the red stain of light from the Triplex. A frozen
dinner. The Scotch bottle. I swallowed hard and
headed inside.

I rode up the elevator. Slogged down the hall. I
reached out with my key to unlock my apartment
door.

Then I stopped. I stared at the door. My free hand
drifted up to my throat. I felt the fading mark of the
wire.

I reached out again, turned the lock slowly. Turned
the knob slowly. Pushed the door in, standing back. I
edged closer to the opening, reached around the
jamb. Flicked up the light switch. Kicked the door in
with my foot. There was no one in the room in front
of me. But I stepped in quickly, looked quickly to
either side. Checked behind the door. Peered into
the kitchenette. No one.

"You jackass," I said aloud.

I kicked the door shut behind me.

I yanked my tie open as I went to the kitchenette.
I collected some ice in a glass. Collared the Scotch
bottle. Headed for my desk.

I dropped into my chair. Dashed out a shot of
liquor. I was aching for it again. Wound tight inside.
Eager to feel its heat break the hold of the day.

I set the bottle down on the desk. Tossed my
cigarette pack beside it. Leaned back and threw my
feet up next to both. I sipped the Scotch and felt it
burn its way into me. I watched the red glow of the

Triplex on the face of the night. I watched my own reflection staring at me.

And I heard footsteps at my back.

They started in the bedroom. They came slowly, calmly out through the bedroom door. I didn't turn. I kept looking in the window. The footsteps stopped directly behind me.

I stuck a cigarette between my teeth. I lit it. "You better have a gun," I said.

I heard a laugh. "Sure, I got a gun. Every cop's got a gun."

I tilted my head to one side.

"Aw shit," I said.

Next to my reflection now, I saw the wavering image of Tom Watts.

I shook my head, disgusted. "I thought your weapon of choice was a dump truck."

He laughed again. I could hear his lip curl. He took a few more steps around the room, looking it over.

I smoked my cigarette, drank my drink. Maybe if I ignored him, he'd go away.

"Shitty little place you've got here, Wells."

"We can't all shake down hookers, Tommy. Some of us just get by."

"A big-shot journalist like you oughta be able to strangle young men in a penthouse, I'd think."

"You're just spoiled by years of the pad." I blew smoke at the window. "Hey, by the way, you wouldn't happen to have a search warrant on you, would you?"

"Gee, I had one here a minute ago." He tapped

the pockets of his trenchcoat. Then shrugged, smiled. "What's a few civil liberties between friends?"

"Nothing. But we're not friends. Get out." I pulled my feet off the desk. I swiveled around in the chair. "And try not to leave a trail of slime."

He grinned. I saw his teeth. He shook a finger at me. "Now, I don't want to have to break your arms, John."

"I don't want to have to call my lawyer."

"I met your lawyer, I don't blame you." He snorted. His green eyes caught the light, and the handsome face went wicked. He stuck a cigarette in it. As he lifted the match to it, his coat opened. He did have a gun, at that. He waved the match out. "Look, Wells," he said. "We oughta talk."

"You talk. I'm drinking."

"Sure. Fine. I'll talk." He ran a thumb over his lip. Thought it over. He looked a little reluctant to get started. As if this wasn't as much fun as, say, handcuffing a guy to a desk leg and then grinding a heel into his mouth. Finally, though, he nodded and said: "Okay. The way I see it, your position is this: upside down in shit to your ankles. I'm in a fair way to have you indicted for murder two and, frankly, nothing would make me a happier guy. But I'm not like you, John. I can't think about revenge all the time."

"Well," I said modestly, "I don't have to worry about greed and corruption."

He shook his head, tapped an ash off onto my floor. Stared down at it. "The thing is: I might be willing to save the taxpayers some money—your trial, your bread and board, that sort of thing—if you thought you could find it in your heart to shut your fucking face up about E. J. McMahon."

He stopped, let it hang there. Gazed at me with his green eyes, gauging my reaction.

I let him sweat, took a drag. Then I smiled at him. He smiled at me. I wagged my head. He wagged his. I chuckled. He chuckled back.

I said: "Good. That's good."

"You like that?"

"Yeah. I do. It's sharp."

"Hey. Happy to amuse."

"The commissioner can shut me up long enough for you to bust me. But if you bust me, I'll bring in E.J. as a defense. Might even prove it."

"I doubt it."

"But it's a possibility."

"Anything's possible."

"Right. Right." I laughed some more. He laughed some more, too.

"No one's listening to you, Wells," he said pleasantly. "Why waste your time? Why waste the ink?"

"Damned if I know."

"There you go."

"It's, like, a complex."

"Doctors can do a lot for those nowadays."

"I mean, sometimes—sometimes I lie awake at night, and I think about some guy, you know, out in the boroughs. Working some shop somewhere, pulling twenty grand, thirty grand. Couple of kids, thinking about college. And paying a big hunk of every dime he makes to the City of New York. And then," I went on, "I think about you. Selling that badge he bought you to the same bunch of scumbags who bleed his union and sell his kids dope and murder each other on his streets. I'm serious, Tommy. I lie awake."

"That's not good, John. A man needs his sleep."

"I mean, let me ask you something: Did you ever arrest anyone? Just out of curiosity."

Watts was still smiling, but the smile had frozen. It looked sharp, feral. His eyes gleamed. "You know," he said, "I'm really beginning to worry about you."

"That's sweet. I'm touched."

"I mean it. I really am. A man who kills a respected citizen is in a precarious position."

I drank. I watched him over the rim of the glass.

"Pretty soon, you're going to be wanted for murder," he said. "A dangerous business. You could be blown away resisting arrest. Or you could get depressed and hang yourself in a holding cell. Or Rikers . . ." He pursed his lips, shook his head. "Ooh, that bad, bad Rikers. I hate to think what might happen to you there if one of your fellow inmates took a dislike to you. Life, in such situations, can be a harsh and uncertain thing. I worry about you, John. Sincerely."

He looked at me hard. I set my drink down on the desk behind me. I stood up, my cigarette clenched in my teeth. I sent his look back at him through the smoke.

"Kill the McMahon story," he said.

"Your badge is mine, Tommy. You're mine." It did not sound like my voice.

For a minute, Watts didn't react. He kept standing

there, looking at me, as if I hadn't spoken. Then he dropped his cigarette on my floor. Right on the spot where Thad Reich died. He crushed it under his heel.

"That's one thing I can count on with you, Wells," he said. "You're a real idiot. Sort of restores my faith in journalism." He started for the door. But he paused with his hand on the knob. "Remember I gave you this chance, though. It's a last chance. Your time is just about up."

"If you had something, you'd use it," I said.

His eyes flashed angrily at that. "Yeah, maybe. Maybe I don't have anything yet. But it's lined up, Wells."

"Sure it is."

He yanked the door open. "It's lined up and ready. A witness. Someone who can connect you to Reich. Someone who can supply your motive." He smiled. "I'll be back. So—sweep the floor, would you?"

He slammed the door shut behind him. I was free to start drinking in earnest.

16

The next time I opened my eyes, it was another day. Sunday, I think. I was lying on top of my bed. The bed was still made. I was still dressed. It's the fastest way to start your morning.

I rolled over, tried to sit up. The motion made the room swirl. I lay back down. I stared at the ceiling. Slowly, the swirling stopped.

I did better on the second try. I actually had myself on the edge of the bed. I stumbled to the bathroom, clutching my stomach. Then out into the living room, clutching my head.

I managed to make myself a mug of coffee. I stuck a frozen waffle in the oven and sat at the kitchenette counter, drinking. I stared at the spot on the floor where Tom Watts's cigarette lay. Soon, I smelled char and got the waffle out. I sat at the counter and stared at the cigarette. I munched on the waffle. I drained the mug. The waffle and coffee rolled around in my stomach. I had a smoke. It sat in my lungs.

I passed the time that way till nearly ten. Then I fell over to my desk chair, dropped into it. Plucked up the receiver and dialed the paper.

"City room."

"Ray. This is Wells."

"Wells! Sorry to hear your career is finished and your life is ruined."

"Thanks."

"What else is new?"

"I'm looking for Howard Baumgarten's home number. You got it lying around someplace?"

"Yeah, it's probably in the computer."

"Well, can you open the computer and take it out in some recognizable form, because . . ."

"Here it is. You want his I'm-a-good-citizen number in the city or the place in Westchester where he lives?"

"Gimme Westchester."

He read it off to me.

"Give me his address, too."

"He won't talk to you from there, you know. He won't admit it exists. I once called him and he pretended to be a machine."

"It's a step up from a cog."

"Right."

There was a pause. I rubbed my eyes. "So how's the weather in there?"

"Cold, my friend, with a chance of suspension by tomorrow. They were upstairs Friday afternoon chewing you over but good. Bush all but called you a murderer. 'This squalid little killing,' he called it. So the new girl—Walsh—she's in there like Joe Louis. Bim. Bam. She's telling him: I'm in charge of the city-room operations and if you wanted someone you could push around, you hired the wrong woman, this and that, blah, blah, blah."

"To Bush?"

"Yeah."

I laughed. "To Bush?"

Ray giggled wildly. "Not bad for her first week. And Sandler is saying, 'I think if we take another look at this . . .' And Hodgekiss is going, 'Now, Emma. Now, Emma.' And finally . . ."

"Wait a minute. Where do you get this stuff?"

"I got a source up in Accounting."

"Who, her? You lucky son of a bitch."

"Good ears, too."

"Damn. So what happened?"

"Well, Bush said he'd take another look at the thing, but from the way it sounded, he just wanted to get Walsh out of there so he could dump you without the noise. He may not get a chance like this again."

"Especially if they hang me."

"Right."

"Thanks, Ray."

"'Bye."

I hung up. Went into the bathroom. Washed up, showered. Stood over the toilet, feeling sick, trying not to puke. I went back to the bedroom and sat on the edge of the bed again. I took long, even breaths, hoping to get steady, hoping I would get by.

I was weary of it by now, of feeling sick, of drinking. Weary of the badgering of voices. Weary of the guilt. Man, but I wished Thad Reich was alive again. In fact, I sat there wishing it for several moments. He went on being dead.

I gave up. Went back to the desk. Back to the

phone. I dialed Baumgarten. His wife answered. I tried to sound friendly.

"Mrs. Baumgarten?"

"Yes?"

"Hi. Is Howard there?"

"Who's calling, please?"

"This is Mikki Snow."

"Just a moment."

I waited, smoking. Looked out the window. The sky had cleared. It was a light, crystal blue. Small clouds were blowing across it. The quiet of a spring Sunday drifted up to me.

"Listen, Miss Snow." It was the deep, curt, gravelly voice of the city's comptroller. "If you have business to conduct with me, you'll have to do it in my office." I waited, to see if he'd go on. "Hello?"

"This is John Wells, Howard."

There was a pause. "You son of a bitch. Where are you calling from?"

"My voting address."

"You have the wrong number."

"I want to know about Mikki Snow."

"Damn it!" He breathed fiercely a moment. Then: "Meet me downtown in an hour and a half."

I pulled my ear away from the slam of the phone.

I spent the next ninety minutes or so at the Greek diner with coffee and the Sunday papers. A melee at a rock concert had the front page. There was nothing new on the Thad Reich story. Both the *Star* and the *News* kept the investigation close to the front. If the *Times* ran something, I couldn't find it.

Around noon, I took the subway down to Brooklyn

Bridge. I came out into the silence of Sunday at City Hall Park. The place was deserted. Only a beggar or two shuffled through the common across the street. All around, the monumental marble buildings rose, and hardly a car went by them. Hardly a person passed. The breeze whipped through the colonnades, under the pediments and arches, up and down the sweeping stairs. The air smelled of honeysuckle.

I walked the few steps to the Municipal Building. An impressive old skyscraper, a massive arcade on the street, then a long winged tower up to columned spires against the sky. "Civic Fame" stands at the very top of it. I've never known her to go in.

Neither did I. As I walked under the arcade, heading toward the doors, a long black limousine pulled up to the curb behind me. I turned, waited, in shadow, flanked by enormous pillars, overhung by the vaulted ceiling. The rear door of the car swung open. Howard Baumgarten stepped out.

He was a big, burly man, a head taller than me and broad across. He seemed to stretch the limits of his tailored gray suit. He was bald and sharp-featured and deep-eyed like an eagle. He had a cigar clenched in his teeth.

He strode up to me. "You son of a bitch," he croaked. "You don't know squat."

"Let's talk about Mikki Snow," I said.

"You don't know squat about Mikki Snow. You don't know squat about anything."

"Why did you lobby for Cooper House?"

"And I'll tell you something else, you two-bit shark, you're going down for murder, and soon, too. And that means you're going to come up before a judge. And that means someone who owes the party a favor. And that means your ass. You and your cheap tricks and your... cheap suit."

"You son of a bitch. This is a great suit."

He stuck his cigar at my chest. "You know," he said, "I've never liked you, Wells. You think just because you're honest you're some kind of hero. You oughta try working for the City sometime. A lot of people in this town are gonna dance the day you're indicted. You don't have friends. You know that? You don't have any friends." Suddenly, he seemed to grow thoughtful. He narrowed his eyes as if he were sizing me up. He leaned back on his heels, still pointing with a kind of sleepy rhythm. "I could fix that for you, you know. Fix you up with people. A good PR firm somewhere. Lot of money in that. Lot of contracts I could send your way. Big contracts, glamour stuff. Double your salary, I'd bet. Triple it, if you play it right."

"Come on, Howard, what the hell is it with you and this place? Why did you lobby for Celia Cooper? The fix was in."

"Ah!" He waved me off. "You don't know anything. You're cheap and you're stupid and you don't know anything." He spun around and started walking away. His hulking body was framed in the arching entranceway, set against the grass of the park, the blue sky, the scuds of clouds merrily passing. He walked to the very edge of the arcade, until he became a silhouette.

"Where's Mikki Snow?" I said.

He spun around again and came stomping back to me. He replanted his cigar in my chest. "I don't like that. I don't like you asking me that. How the hell should I know where she is?"

"She came to see you."

"You don't know that."

"But she did, didn't she?"

He put the cigar in his mouth for a moment. Chewed the soggy end, thinking. Then he growled: "Yeah. Okay. Say she did."

"What did she want?"

"How the hell should I know? She was a book-keeper. She wanted to double-check the amount of a grant or something."

"With the comptroller?"

"With my staff. She came to see my staff."

"What are we, making this up as we go along?"

"I came out of the office, that's all. I came out and said hello. I shook her hand. I'm never too busy to help the homeless." Even he couldn't keep a straight face. He laughed. "Heh heh heh." He leaned back, stuck his gray vest out at me, chomped on his cigar again. "Heh heh heh."

I shook my head. "Now she's gone."

"Don't know anything about it."

"Haven't seen her?"

"Don't know anything about it." He stuck a thumb under the vest's armholes. He tilted his bald head back, peered over the top of mine.

"You still under investigation for that kickback scheme? How many jobs do you control, anyway? A thousand?"

It sounded desperate to me, too. And Baumgarten just broke into a big grin. He laid his scaly hand on my shoulder. He spoke around his cigar. "You make life so hard on yourself, Wells. Everything could be so easy. You got a little problem with Tommy Watts? We can smooth it over. You need a little breathing space from the D.A.? It can be done. This is New York, John. It's a city of possibilities. I meant what I said about that PR job."

I gazed up at his eagle face. I gazed down at his scaly hand. He let go of me.

He plucked the cigar from his mouth and pointed it at me one last time.

"I meant what I said about that judge, too. That's a cardinal rule in politics, you know: never get tried by a stranger." When I didn't say anything, he cocked his head regretfully, sighed. "Too bad. I always knew you were an asshole."

Once again, he moved toward the street, toward the shiny black limo parked at the curb. His footsteps echoed up and down the arcade.

At his car, he paused. He adjusted his jacket, staring off at the blue sky over City Hall Park. He glanced back at me again. "Arrivederci, Wells," he said.

"This is a great suit," I called after him.

"Ah . . ." He waved me off. He slid into the car. The door shut softly. It glided away.

For another moment, I stood there, under the towering ceiling. Then I lit a cigarette, moved toward the arch as well. When I stepped out into the light, I glanced up just as Baumgarten had. I saw the square of grass, the trees reaching up, laying a lacework of branches in front of City Hall's dome. I saw the statue of Horace Greeley, a rumpled bronze seated out in front of the old Tweed Courthouse.

And just beyond Greeley, I saw a flash of motion. I watched and saw a man swerve out from behind the statue. He was hurrying away.

He was small, slim. Wore jeans and a windbreaker. He jogged toward the weathered gray marble courthouse. The sun gleamed on his blond hair.

I waited. I watched him go, waiting for him to look back. But he never did. A second more and he vanished behind the building. He was gone.

I hadn't had a good look at him. I hadn't seen his face at all. I couldn't be positive from that distance.

But I thought—I was almost certain—that it had been Mark Herd.

17

"Give me Sam Scar."

"Who's calling, please?"

"His brother: Ugly."

I held the line while she went to find him. I put my finger in my ear. I was standing in a booth in a Chinese restaurant off Mott Street. The voices and clattering plates of the Sunday dim sum crowd made it tough to hear.

Scar came on. "Who's this?"

"It's Wells. Can you talk?"

"Yeah. Yeah. Go ahead."

"I need to get into the Cooper House offices."

"They're not open now. This is the upstairs."

"Yeah, I figured that. That's what I need."

"Uh oh. How come?"

"Because..." A waiter with a tray went by, screaming out the name of a dish.

"Yo," said Scar. "Get me some of that."

"Because something's down in the cellar. That's why Herd's been getting all your jobs. You can work on the stove 'cause that's upstairs, but the compactor and the boiler..."

"The circuit breakers, yeah..."

"Ever since Mikki Snow's been gone, you've been kept from going downstairs."

"Shit, I never thought of that."

"Neither did I, till a few minutes ago. I think maybe Mikki Snow found something down there or hid something...I don't know. Maybe if we find it—I get what I want, you get what you want. Like I said, I don't know."

I listened while Sam Scar thought it over on the other end. Then he started speaking—but a clattering tower of dishes rolled past.

"What?"

"I say it's hot. Here," he said. "Today. The man's been around."

"Watts?"

"Yeah. He was in there with her."

"With Celia."

"Yeah. She usually stays home on Sunday, but she came in special today and they talked in the office. He's gone now, though."

"What about her?"

"She's getting ready to leave."

"Can you get me in?"

"Shit, man." He thought again. "It'd have to be soon. Come dinner, they open for the tickets. At night, they got a guard in the hall. Three to five's the best time."

"How about in an hour?"

"Yeah. But you gotta be there on the dot. Wait out of sight till I open the door, then come in a hurry. I'll let you in." I heard him sigh. Then he said: "How you get out—that I don't know."

An hour later, I was in front of Cooper House again. This time, I stood across the street. There was a restaurant there, with a recessed kitchen door. I stood in the alcove, the smell of steak seeping out to me through the door's metal. I leaned one shoulder against the brick wall, smoked a cigarette, waited. I kept my eye on the chiseled tower that rose against the blue sky. I watched its huge wooden entrance. On the sidewalk in front of me, an old woman wobbled past, tugged by her dog. I nodded to her. A cute redhead with two cute redheaded girls hurried down the hill. I tipped a finger from my brow. It wasn't a great hiding place, but it beat crouching behind a tree.

Finally, the wooden doors opened. I tossed my cigarette, straightened. Sam Scar's bullet head poked out into the open. He looked this way and that.

I broke from the alcove, jogged across the street.

"You supposed to be hiding," he whispered.

"I was hiding, that was hiding."

"Shit."

"Would you let me in?"

He stood back and I slipped inside. He shut the door behind me.

"Someone see us, I get my ass fired. Come on."

The spacious hall was lighted by the chandelier, but there were no people there, no sound. Silence from the drop-in center to my right. Silence from the stairs against the far wall. The door to the offices was shut. I followed Scar to it.

"Now, we got a problem," he said. He bent over the doorknob, rummaging through the keys on a large ring. "Shit, we got lots of problems, two big ones." He cast a nervous eye toward the stairs. "Number one, the keys. You gotta take the keys in with you to open the cellar door—and *I* gotta get them back to Security before they missed. That means you got fifteen minutes in there, no more." He found the key, slipped it into the lock. Froze at a shout from upstairs. Waited, his mouth open, his eyes wide. Then, when the silence came down to us, he opened the lock, pushed in the door.

"What's number two?" I asked.

He looked at me, his face close to mine. I could feel his breathing hard and hot. I could see the fresh wound on his cheek, nestled black in the crevice of his old scar.

"About two minutes after you called, Celia went out," he said. "She said she got a call on her inside line, said it was an emergency. She said she'd have to come back to finish up her work. Could be anytime."

I looked through the open door into the office. Saw the shape of furniture standing dead and silent in the light from the window.

"Damn," I said.

"So you got fifteen minutes—or not. One or the other. I'll go into drop-in and keep an eye out." He slipped the keys into my hand.

"Thanks, Scar."

"Yeah," he said. "Shit."

I went through the door. Scar eased it shut behind me.

The quiet and the dark closed in at once. Not total quiet. Not total dark. There were plenty of sounds from the street just beyond the window. The whisper of cars, the rumble of them from the avenue, voices of people passing, a barking dog. And there was daylight: soft, sunless afternoon light falling over everything.

But in here, the life of the street, the light of the day, seemed out of reach. In here, the desks were all neat, and the chairs tucked in under them. The phones were silent, the lamps off. In here, the nearby noise and light had a distant, kind of sad quality to it, like birds heard from a prison cell.

It was a long room, big enough for six desks in two rows of three. There were two doors at the far end, one in the wall facing me, the other to the right. I moved slowly up the aisle between the desks, looking back over my shoulder sometimes, feeling the room's emptiness like a presence following after me.

The door facing me led to Celia Cooper's office. I pushed it in, peered through the crack. It was a tidy place, a square with a big wooden desk in the center. There were lots of pictures on the wall, some of Celia with a woman who looked like her sister, a few of the sister with husband and kids, a few others. I pulled out and went to the other door, the door to my right.

That was the one I was looking for. A cramped cubicle. The desk took up the whole thing. There were white shelves built into the walls, with folders piled into them and stacked on top of them, and dated ledger books slanting this way and that, out of order. There were a couple of public-service posters framed under glass. And there was a door, the door to the cellar. I stepped across the room to it.

It took me a second to find the key, another to work it in the old-fashioned dead bolt. But then the door swung in and I saw the stairs. They were chipped, dirty concrete stairs. They led down into blackness, disappeared in it. I found a light switch on the wall, flicked it up. The hard yellow light of a bare bulb went on down there. I saw a small patch of concrete floor, broken into pebbles. I went down to it.

The cellar was a tangled maze of hallways that seemed to go off in every direction. All of them seemed to end in shadow. I glanced at my watch. Ten minutes left, I figured. But that nervous sense—of being followed, of being watched—made me feel the crush of time. I took a deep breath, listened to it tremble as I let it out. I headed down the hall to my left.

My fingers trailed over the rough concrete wall as I walked toward the dark end. There was an entranceway. I peered in until my eyes adjusted. I saw the compactor, the black bag stretching from the metal tube. I turned, headed back the way I came.

I went down another hall, following a loud hum. I found the boiler, a tangle of pipes twisting around a husky mass in the dark. I turned and went back. Down another hall to find an old dumpster standing by another entrance. I opened the lid of the dumpster, looked in. There were chunks of concrete in there, and a few planks of plasterboard. It looked as if someone had been doing some light construction. I reached in and shifted some of the stones and boards around with my hand. Then I pulled my head out, closed the lid.

I peeked in the entrance. There was a trunk room, stacked high with old boxes and crates. Anything could have been hidden in there. I would never have found it—but then, neither would Sam Scar in the normal course of things, and there would've been no reason to keep him out.

I shook my head, took a look at my watch again. "Damn," I whispered.

Time was almost up. I turned and walked quickly back to the stairs. At the foot of them, under the light of the bare bulb, I paused for a second to dust off my hands. I paused—and then I stopped cold.

My hands were covered with dust. Dust from the plasterboard, dust from the stones. They were white boards, white stones. It should have been white dust.

But some of it was brown. There were flecks of brown on my palm. It looked like dried blood.

I glanced at my watch again. My fifteen minutes were gone. I headed back down the hall to the dumpster.

I found a light switch just inside the trunk room, flicked it on. In the outglow, I opened the dumpster lid again. Reached in. Rummaged through the stones and boards—and found what I was looking for.

A board. A two-by-four. And one edge of it was stained a dark rusty brown. Deeply stained, too, as if something had been seeping into it for a long time. When I rubbed my thumb over the surface of it, brown dust and flecks came off—and there was still more brown underneath. When I laid the board back, I saw other boards and a stone or two that had also been touched by the stain.

I reached in deep, pulled up more stones. More and more, until I could see the dumpster's bottom. But that was it. There was nothing else there.

I looked at the thing another second, my brain running over the possibilities. But I couldn't stay. I'd been in the cellar almost twenty minutes now. I had to get out, get back to Scar with the keys. I flicked the lights off, walked quickly to the stairs. Jogged up them. Hit the lights. Slipped back into the little room where Mikki Snow had worked. Closed and locked the cellar door. Went toward the outer office...

But I never got that far. I was stopped by a picture, one of the photos on the wall. I hadn't noticed it before: it was a group shot taken in front of Cooper House. Celia was at the center of it, with Thad Reich on one side of her and Mark Herd on the other. Sam Scar was in back of Reich, a hand on his shoulder. And standing next to Sam, there was a young woman. She was pretty, in her early twenties, I'd say, with dark brown skin and black, black hair swept straight back. She had a high forehead and big, melting brown eyes that made her smile look sort of wistful and brave.

I thought of Mikki Snow, who had come to New York to look for work and "got homeless" instead. Celia Cooper's bookkeeper, who'd had some business with Howard Baumgarten. Now she was gone, and the cellar was off limits and there was a stain down there, a stain too much like blood.

I stood still in the room and looked around me. Ran my eyes over the stacks of folders, the rows of books. Mikki Snow had worked here, going over the records, the finances... I reached out and pulled a ledger off the shelf. It was a huge book, oversize, heavy. It was dated six years ago. I hefted it in two hands, set it on the desk. I opened it, looked down a page. Flipped through a few more.

The book listed the contributions to the place: the sources, the dates, the amounts. It listed the uses of the money: salaries, maintenance, food, and so on. The operation looked pretty simple, two large city grants, some money from the state for drug counseling, one or two foundations weighing in with large donations. There was plenty of white space on the book's big pages.

I closed the book quietly. Hoisted it again. Started to slip it back onto its shelf.

Then the light went on in the outer office. It leaked in underneath the door. I went rigid, still holding the ledger in my hands.

I heard movement out there. Footsteps muffled in the carpeting. Breathing slowly, I continued sliding the book onto its shelf.

There was a soft metallic click. I looked over my shoulder. The doorknob was turning. I shoved the book into place, moved back to the cellar door.

And my shoulder brushed against another ledger. It tottered as I turned to it, fell from the shelf.

Landed with a thud that made the floor shudder. It splayed open on two pages filled from top to bottom in a cramped, careful hand, and while I stared down at it, the door was pulled open.

Then I raised my eyes, still staring, into the fierce eyes staring back.

18

"I would have thought you had more brains, Mr. Wells."

I sat on the edge of the desk, closed my eyes, pinched the bridge of my nose.

When I looked up, Celia Cooper was picking up the ledger on the floor. She looked at me over the top of it. She clapped it shut. Dumped it heavily back on a shelf.

"Find anything?" she asked me.

I shook my head.

Her eyes flared. Her lips were white. An angry red flush appeared on her cheeks in splotches. Her fists were clenched at her sides. Her arms trembled and her eyes glistened with raging tears.

"I did not deserve this," she said. She managed to keep her voice even. "I did not deserve this from you."

I could not speak at all. I nodded.

"I talked to you," she went on. "Even after you killed my friend, I did what I could. I tried to help you. I did not deserve this... violation of... of my *rights*."

I stood up, put my hands in my pockets. "Miss Cooper, I didn't mean to violate—"

"You didn't mean!" Now the red came up into her cheeks completely. Now the tears were brimming over, the white lips quivering. "You didn't mean to . . . to kill Thad. You didn't mean to break into my property. Suppose I call the police and explain to them what you didn't mean to do."

"Miss Cooper, I was looking for a woman, an employee of yours named Mikki Snow. I'd heard—"

"Oh!" Celia Cooper brought her clenched fist to her mouth. The tears spilled down her cheeks. She shook her head angrily. "What was Mikki Snow to you?" she said.

"She might've—"

"Did you know her?" Her face was contorted, her voice was savage.

"No, but—"

"Had you ever even met her?"

"I thought she—"

"Because *I* did. *I* knew her. I knew her very well." She ran her hand up through the graying ringlets of her hair. She shook her head—and her eyes were drawn, as mine had been, to the photograph on the wall. She looked at it as she spoke, and I thought about the young woman in it and her soft, sad, courageous smile. "I took her out of the shelters when she'd been raped and beaten," Celia said. "And I sat on her bed while she nearly died of the drugs she took for . . . for some kind of stupid, stupid comfort. And I held her while she vomited again and again and while she was racked and twisted with convulsions. I did all that."

She turned from the picture, faced me. I couldn't look into those angry eyes anymore. I bowed my head.

Celia Cooper's voice dropped to a hoarse whisper. "And I found the intelligence in there and . . . and the spirit of the woman—still in there after everything, Mr. Wells. And I put her on the track to being free, to being . . . *somebody* again, and now . . ."

I glanced at her. "Now what? What happened?"

She covered her face with her hand, turned from me. "Oh, go away," she said. "You're not even worth calling the police over. They'll take care of you soon enough. I don't know . . . who you are, or why you did what you did . . . but you've brought nothing to this house but bad luck and tragedy and . . ." Now when she faced me, those deep, soft brown eyes of hers had gone cold and black. "I can't forgive you. I tried. I can't. I never will. I want nothing but to see you punished for what you did, for what you're still doing. Go on!" She flung a hand out, accidentally knocking a stack of folders off a shelf to the floor. "Go on, and search for your dirt. If you can find it, then find it and try to save yourself, try to use it as a reason for killing Thad." She leaned toward me, her cheeks dry now, her gaze terrible. "But I'll tell you something, Mr. Wells. I'll tell you something that's true. The world is a very ugly place, a very awful place, and all corrupt—but there *is* such a thing as justice. And if I've done some things to keep this place alive, if I've made some deals and learned some ropes so that my brother and sister human beings didn't have to live without hope and shelter and dignity—then believe me, I have paid the price for that, paid it and paid it. And no matter what you find out, no matter how you use it or twist it or turn it around, you'll pay for what you did, too. You'll pay in full. I'll see to it. Now, get out of here."

She waved her arm at me. Like shooing a bee. But I didn't move. I said: "What happened? What happened to Mikki Snow?"

For a long moment, she just stared at me. Then she swallowed hard and said softly: "She's gone." Her voice broke. "She's gone forever."

"Why?"

Moving away from me, moving to the wall, to the picture on the wall, she made a helpless gesture. "I don't know. How should I know? Maybe because ... she wanted me to be more ... or better ... than I am."

"Do you know where she went?"

"Oh yes. Oh yes, I know." She leaned against the wall, her eyes only inches from the photograph. "I just got back from there," she said softly. "I was the only one they knew to call."

"From where? Who called you?"

"The police. They found her in an SRO on Thirty-second Street. They wanted me to identify her."

"In jail?"

"No. At the morgue." She reached up, gently touched the photo's frame. "It was an overdose, they said."

19

I went back to my apartment. I sat in the chair at my desk. I smoked a cigarette. The Scotch bottle was on the kitchenette counter. I eyed it from across the room.

The long last hour of the afternoon drifted toward evening. The sky began to darken at the window. I sat. I smoked. I tried to think. I could not think.

There was nothing left to think about, no way left for me to go. If Mikki Snow had ever been a lead, she was gone now. If her death of an overdose in a fourth-class dive meant anything, I couldn't figure out what. Maybe it happened the way Celia Cooper said. Maybe Snow had killed herself because she'd become disillusioned with her savior, with Cooper. Maybe she'd found some sort of scam at Cooper House, or simply witnessed the compromises Cooper had made with the city. Or maybe it wasn't that at all. Maybe the pull of the drug had just become too much. But whatever it was, it didn't really seem to matter. None of it explained why Thad Reich had been in my apartment. None of it gave him a motive for attacking me. And none of it gave me a reason to kill him.

The world is an awful place, said Celia Cooper, *but there is such a thing as justice*.

A man was dead, after all. Someone had to pay.

I reached for the ashtray, jabbed out my cigarette. I lit another. Kept studying the whiskey bottle on the counter. After a while, I got up, wandered over to it. Picked it up by the neck, read the label. It was Scotch, all right. I set it down and walked to the window.

The sky was purple now. The air was cool and easy. The store lights glared up from the street below. Cars raced past—not many, yellow cabs mostly. The sidewalks were busier: lots of people went strolling by. Couples with their arms linked, women walking dogs, men with their hands in their pockets, their newspapers under their arms—all of them passed along, unconcerned, content with their spring Sunday on the island of Manhattan.

I pressed my cigarette to my lips and watched them go. I knew they were not really the way they seemed to me just then. They were worried, most of them, afraid, obsessed, even half-mad—they were New Yorkers, weren't they? But from where I stood, they seemed a serene fraternity: the brotherhood of those who had not killed anyone, who lived pretty much on the right side of the law. It felt like a million years since I'd been one of them. I never would be one of them again.

The door buzzer sounded. A coppery taste of fear came into my mouth. The buzzer sounded again.

I went to the intercom.

"Who is it?"

A woman's voice answered through the static: "It's me. Back in your life."

I put my hand on the release, but didn't press it. I almost called down again. Then I let her in.

I stood at the open door, finished my cigarette while I waited for the elevator. Finally, I heard it rumble to the floor, ease to a stop. The doors slid open.

Kathy Reich stepped out.

She wore red and yellow this time. Expensive stuff: a scarlet skirt down to her ankles, a yellow sweater with a cowl neck. A gold choker gleamed at her throat. A small black leather purse was strung over her shoulder.

She turned in the hall to face me, arced her hand on her wrist by way of salute. I arced my hand back.

Her glossed lips curled as she slowly stepped toward me. "I figure it this way," she said. "Either you're telling the truth, or you have testicles the size of bowling balls. Which is it?"

"Tough to choose."

"I mean, you don't go to a guy's wife, for Christ's sake, after you've murdered him. I mean, it's pretty lame: Hi, I killed your husband, could you give me a hand beating the rap. Unless you're a criminal mastermind or something, and you don't exactly strike me as Professor Moriarty. I mean, no offense, but even Mr. Wizard is, like, stretching it."

She leaned against the wall.

"Why don't you come in?" I said.

With a glance over my shoulder into the apartment, she shook her head. "I don't think so. I mean, I know he's not still in there, but..."

"Okay. Sure."

She took a deep breath, avoided my gaze. "You wouldn't happen to have a cigarette, would you?"

I gave her one. She watched me through the smoke as I lit it for her.

"Thanks," she said. She plucked it from her lips, held it upright. "I'm giving them up. That's why I'm not carrying mine, I mean. Obviously, I'm not giving them up to the point of not smoking them, but I figure at a time like this the stress'll probably kill me before the smoke does. I figure if I can sort of cut down through the grief stages—like a pack for Denial, a half-pack during Anger—by Acceptance, I should be home free. Anyway, if I blow it, who can blame me, so it's a pretty safe arena. Thad had a lover, you know. Not that that has anything to do with the cigarettes, but it might explain a few things for you. I don't know what. But I thought I'd tell you." She dragged on her cigarette from the corner of her mouth, watching me.

I started to speak. Behind me, the phone rang. Kathy Reich went on.

"I mean, he wasn't exactly Stanley Kowalski, in the first place, don't get me wrong..."

The phone rang.

"...he didn't stand outside on the street screaming 'Kathy, Kathy' all night, but I mean, Jesus, now and then I used to get what we politely call laid, thank you very much..."

The phone rang. I didn't even glance back at it. I didn't want her to stop.

"... not that that was any great shakes, but it had a certain intimacy to it because, of course, it was sex, which is what that's like, but after Cooper House..."

The phone rang.

"... conjugal-bliss-wise we were at ground zero. I said, 'Thad, you don't have to trade IBM to turn me on, I'll put out, I'm your wife, for Christ's sake,' but after a while, I mean, comes the dawn, you start to get wise.... Shouldn't you answer that?"

The phone rang. I hesitated, then turned and headed for the desk. The phone began to ring again—but stopped in the middle of the bell. My hand fell onto the receiver. The phone was silent. I turned back to her.

She was not leaning on the wall now. She was standing straight. She was holding her purse in one hand in front of her, as if for protection. She was staring at the floor of my apartment.

"I'm standing here telling the man who crushed my husband's windpipe about my sex life," she said. "Good, Kath. Nice going. Is that where he died?" She gestured at the floor with her cigarette.

I glanced at the spot. It was right where he died. "I ... I don't ..."

"Take it slow, Wells. One word at a time."

"I don't know exactly. I was kind of dazed from the fight."

"Right there, huh?"

"Yeah."

"Whew. I'm glad I don't have to live here. Bet it's a blast."

"It does have its bad moments."

She took another long look at the floor, then nodded to herself, as if she were ready to leave.

Quickly, I moved back to her. "Did he tell you?" I asked her. "Did he tell you he was having an affair?"

"What? Oh. You want to hear the rest of this? Yeah, he did. That's the whole point, in fact. That's what I came here to tell you. We had this whole big fight about it." She shook her head, smiling wryly. "At this point, you probably think I need a psychiatrist. Actually, I've thought of a psychiatrist, but then I might have to come to terms with my parents—"

The phone on my desk started ringing again.

"I mean, they grow potatoes, for Christ's sake. They live in Idaho. I talk Kafka, they talk spuds. Jesus."

The phone rang.

"What is this with your phone?" she said. "Are you taking a survey?"

"You had a fight," I prompted. "He told you he was having an affair."

The phone rang.

"Look, maybe you better answer that. We could do this another time. I don't even know why I . . . Yeah, that's it. He wanted to go out, and I said, look, you know, once in a while . . ."

The phone rang.

". . . and he . . . he said . . . he told me he loved someone else . . ."

"Did he tell you—"

The phone rang.

"—who it was?" I asked.

Kathy Reich stared past me at the phone on the desk as it rang and rang. "Well, yeah," she murmured. "Sure, that's what hurt. I mean, another guy, that punk, that Mark Herd... I could've stood for that, in some ways. But Celia. Celia Cooper, that self-righteous—"

The phone rang.

"Look," she said, "I've gotta... I've gotta go..." She started moving toward the elevator. "I'm a little confused, I thought I could help. I need some quality personal time here..." She pressed the call button. The car had not gone. The doors slid open at once.

The phone rang again.

"Why did you tell me this?" I asked her. "What does it have to do with me?"

She paused, halfway into the car, her hand holding the door's bumper.

"That's what we were arguing about. That he was going out. I mean, I thought he was going out to meet her, to meet Celia. But it turns out he was coming here, he must have come right here. That was the last time I ever saw him. The last time, and I was screaming and crying and accusing him—the whole bit."

The phone rang. She laughed: a startling, delighted little trill.

"What a life, huh?" she said. "It's a riot." She stepped into the elevator. The doors slid shut. She was gone.

The phone rang.

"Shut up, goddamn it," I said. "Damn!"

I stepped angrily across the room and grabbed it. "What do you want?"

"Wells! Finally!" I knew the voice right off: soft, deep, slightly hoarse, slightly southern. "This is Emma Walsh."

"Emma." I dropped down into my desk chair. I looked out the window. The sky had turned a deep shade of purple, washed by the city lights below. Somewhere in the distance, a siren cried.

"I hear you've been taking it pretty hard for me," I said.

"Jesus, Wells. How'd you get that?"

I laughed. "A perky confidential source."

"That woman in Accounting with the legs, I'll bet. I thought she'd been hanging around the door. Well, I did what I could. But, Wells..." She had to force herself to say it. "It's out of my hands now."

I felt something drop inside me. Like the elevator had gone down too fast. I listened to the siren wailing as Emma tried to speak again.

I managed to speak first. "So you mean I'm suspended?"

I heard her take a deep breath. I heard her let it out in a long sigh.

"No. No, it's not that. Christ, I wish it were that.... Oh, hell, John, I'm so sorry. It just came over the scanner." She paused. Then: "It's Watts. He's issued a warrant for your arrest. You've been charged with murder."

Outside, the siren wailed louder.

<u>20</u>

In another second, the sound peaked. I saw the red light of the police flasher dance over my window-pane. The siren wound down, died.

"Wells?" It was Emma. "Are you still there?"

I laid the receiver on the desk. Stood up. Went to the window. I looked down in the street.

"Wells." Emma's voice came, tinny, from the receiver. "Listen to me. We're going to stick by you all the way."

There were two of them out there. An unmarked car and a cruiser. They pulled up to the curb outside my apartment and parked.

"We're gonna get you a good lawyer," said Emma. "Raise hell. Get bail. You won't have to wait out at Rikers, that's for certain."

I worry about you, Wells.

The door to the unmarked car swung open and out stepped Lieutenant Tom Watts. The cruiser doors popped on either side. Two uniformed patrolmen rolled out.

You could be blown away resisting arrest.

Even in the early dark, I recognized the enormous shape of one of the patrolmen. A slug named Rankin,

Watts's hired troll. It was a good guess the other one wasn't Saint Francis either.

Emma's mechanical voice kept coming to me. "We're going to make this our crusade, John, I promise you. We won't let them get away with it. No bargaining, nothing. We're going to make them prove this thing in a court of law..."

You could hang yourself in a holding cell. Or Rikers—oh, that bad, bad.

Watts paused on the sidewalk to speak to his two patrolmen. Then he and the third cop came marching into my building. Rankin stayed outside. He leaned against his cruiser. He hooked his thumbs in his belt. He lifted his eyes. He gazed directly up at me. He smiled.

"I may have to use up the last of my goodwill," Emma was saying. "But as long as I'm with the paper, at least, you can count on..."

And under her voice, like a sort of static, the other voice continued: *I worry, Wells. Really. I worry.*

I picked up the receiver. I held it to my ear. I felt the vibration of it as my hand shook violently.

"Good-bye, Emma," I said.

"Wells? Wells?"

I hung up on her. I headed for the door.

I figured I didn't have much time. The buzzer in my apartment hadn't rung, but that didn't mean much. Watts could've buzzed the super downstairs. Or just slipped a credit card in the latch, for that matter. Sure enough, when I stuck my head out the door, I could already hear his voice coming from the foyer.

"You take the elevator. I'm going up the stairs."

The other cop answered: "Okay, Lieutenant."

Then I heard the elevator door rattle back four stories below me. And I heard Watts's footstep creak on the bottom rise.

I came out into the hall, closing my door behind me quietly. I hurried across the hall to the only other apartment on my floor. Mrs. Hooterman. An old lady. I didn't know her very well, but I'd grunted a good-morning to her in the hall once or twice. I was sure she'd recognize me, anyway. I rang her doorbell.

There was no answer. Watts's footsteps sounded on the second-floor landing. Started coming up the next flight of stairs. Behind me, the low hum of the elevator grew louder. I rang the doorbell again.

A trembling, cranky voice came through the heavy wood: "I'm comink. Hold your horses."

"Come on, come on," I muttered to the door.

I heard Watts on the third landing, one flight below me. I heard the elevator nearing the fourth floor.

"Ooo is eet?" squeaked Mrs. Hooterman.

"John Wells," I whispered.

"Vat?"

"Wells. Your neighbor. John Wells."

The door opened a crack. I saw sallow eyes in hounddog wrinkles, a cap of blue-white hair. I heard Watts start up the last flight. I heard the elevator ease to a stop behind me.

"Oh, Meester Vells, vat . . . ?"

"I need to borrow a cup of sugar," I said. I pushed

the door in with my shoulder. I nearly bowled Mrs. Hooterman over as I shoved past her into the room.

"Va . . . Va . . . Vere's your cup?" she said.

"I need to borrow a cup, too." I saw the top of Watts's head crest the stairs. I heard the elevator door open. I shut Mrs. Hooterman's door.

I turned around. There she was. A shivering squib of a woman, leaning on a cane. Those eyes regarded me cautiously.

"You need a cup?"

"A cup and sugar. A cup of sugar, in the cup. Right."

I looked around quickly. The layout was pretty much the same as mine. A broad room with the windows on the far wall. Those windows looked out on an alley. Across the alley—about six feet across— was another building: windows in a flat wall of brick.

Mrs. Hooterman had begun vibrating slowly toward the kitchenette.

"Are you bakink a cake?" she called back over her shoulder.

Outside, down the hall, there was pounding on my door.

"Open up, Wells. It's the police."

Mrs. Hooterman paused, turned. "Vat?"

"Huh? Oh, yeah, a cake. Cookies. I'm making cookies. You need sugar for cookies, right?"

"Did ju say somethink about the poleese?"

"Grease. You need grease. Greased sugar cookies. Kids love 'em."

More pounding. "Come on, Wells. We can do this the easy way or the hard way."

Mrs. Hooterman narrowed her eyes at the door. She frowned.

I rushed across the room to the window.

"Come on, Wells," Watts shouted. "Open up. You're covered everywhere."

"Oh mein Gott!" said Mrs. Hooterman.

I threw her window open. Stuck my head out. The air, the city noise, washed over me. There was no fire escape. Just a four-story drop. Across from me—those long six feet away—another window was open to the spring. There was a light on in the apartment, but no one visible.

"Oh mein Gott!" said Mrs. Hooterman again. She started shuffling toward the door.

I climbed out onto the window ledge.

My mouth went suddenly dry as bone. The wind sighed all around me. My throat closed. I breathed in little gasps. I tried not to look down but I sensed the hard pavement of the alleyway below. I sensed it swaying up and down like a ship in a storm.

Behind me, I heard Mrs. Hooterman fumbling with the doorknob. I heard her thin, cracking whine raised in a kind of shout.

"Help! Help, poleese! Oh mein Gott, he's in here, dis creeminal."

I jumped.

There wasn't much push. I could only bend my knees a little, then push off quickly before I lost my balance. After that, for one moment, I was floating through a kind of whirling peacefulness. Only the air surrounded me. The pavement passed by below. The wall of the building ahead drew closer. There was no noise but the city whisper. That single second seemed to stretch out and out and out forever.

Then I slapped into the wall. My cheek crunched against brick. My hand scrabbled blindly for purchase where I thought the open window was. I knew I was about to fall and die. And then I grabbed hold. I wrapped my fingers around the sill, clung until the wood cut my flesh. I hung in the air above the alley, my muscles stretched, my teeth gritted, a steady groan forced out of me in the effort to hold on.

Sobbing, I began to pull myself up. Up the wall toward the window, inch by inch. With a gasp, I threw my arm over the sill. Dragged the lower half of my body up after it.

"Wells!" The patrolman's shout came from across the way. "Stop or I'll shoot!"

Then there was Watts: "For shit's sake. He's getting away. Take him out!"

Another aching effort and I hauled myself over the windowsill. I tumbled into the apartment beyond.

A woman shrieked. I rolled on the floor and looked up in time to see a frying pan come spinning at me through the air. I crossed my arms before my face. The pan struck my wrist. I let out a shout as the pain jolted up and down my arm.

The shriek sounded again. "Don't hurt me! Don't hurt me, please!" A pretty young woman in a blue jogging suit came hurtling through a doorway at me, a butcher knife clutched in both hands. "Don't hurt me, don't hurt me," she screamed. She raised the knife over her head as she barreled toward me.

There was the short snap of a gunshot. The wall

between us exploded in a cloud of white plaster as a bullet tore a hole in it. The woman pulled up short, reared back, still shrieking.

I drove off the floor, flew into her. Tackled her, brought her to the ground as a second shot snapped off, a second cloud of plaster exploded—just where she'd been standing.

"God damn you!" the woman screamed. She tried to drive the butcher knife down into me as we rolled together on the floor. The blade slit the edges of my thumb. I grappled with her, grabbed her wrists, pushed her hands back away from me.

"Mommy! Mommy!"

The woman shrieked: "Simon!"

I raised my head and saw him. A chunky two-year-old waddling through the doorway at full speed, his face contorted with fear.

"Mommy! Mommy!"

"Simon, stay away!" She tried to yank her wrists free.

"Simon stay away!" the child cried. He kept on waddling toward us.

Now I started shrieking, too, babbling as I shrieked: "Tom! Don't shoot, it's a kid, Tom, Tom, Jesus, Tom!" I let the woman go and somersaulted across the room at little Simon. There was another shot. I grabbed the kid. I felt a hot wind burn across the back of my neck. I knocked the kid to the floor and threw my body over him. The wall exploded once again. Chunks of plaster tumbled down from the ceiling.

The woman shrieked: "Who the fuck are the good guys here? I need to know the good guys!" The woman was half off the floor. She was tearing at her hair in panic, her face mottled.

"Get down!" I screamed. "I've got him! Get down!"

The child writhed and shouted in my arms. The mother dropped to the floor. She curled up, her hands to her hair, the knife falling away from her.

For a long moment, we stared at each other, our eyes at floor level, our breath heavy. The shooting had stopped. The quiet was bizarre.

"Mommy?"

"Hush. It's all right," she whispered. She stared at me. "Who's shooting at us?"

"The police."

"Oh no."

"Maa-meeee."

"Hush, sweetie." She choked back her tears.

"It's all right," I told her. "I'm innocent."

"Please don't hurt him, don't hurt my boy," she said.

"I swear. I'm sorry."

"I'll do anything you want."

"Just help me get out of here."

"Don't hurt him, please."

"They'll be coming soon."

"Please."

"Please," I said.

My whole body was shaking. I couldn't stop it. I was gasping for breath. The woman looked desperately at me, at the child squirming and crying in my arms.

I took the kid out from under me, but kept my grip on him. He squirmed, trying to reach his mother. I held him close to the floor. Pushed him across it to her. She reached out, grabbed hold of him, pulled him close. She buried her face in his hair, sobbing.

"Help me," I said. "Please."

She glanced up at me through her tears. "How will they come?"

"The stairs. The elevator. I don't know."

"The door is through there, down the hall." She lifted her chin at the doorway through which she'd entered. "The stairwell goes all the way down to the basement. There's a door down there that leads out to the alley." She held the boy close.

"I'm sorry," I said again.

The woman took a few more breaths. Then she blurted: "The door to the alley is locked. The smallest key on my chain opens it. It's in my purse, hanging on the door."

"Christ," I said. "Thanks, lady."

"You better be the fucking good guy. And drop the keys in the basement when you leave."

"Right. I'm sorry," I said again. She didn't answer. I started crawling on my belly toward the door.

21

In the kitchen, a pot of noodles boiled on the stove. It hissed and overflowed, unattended, in the quiet room. I crawled under it, making my way beneath the windows.

The inches came hard. It hurt to breathe. There was blood running from my hand where the woman had cut it. One of my cheeks had been scraped raw when I'd slammed into the wall. There was pain everywhere. I knew I would not make it all the way.

Slowly, I scrabbled across the floor. After the kitchen, there was a hallway. It was long and dark. There were no windows, so I dragged myself to my feet and started stumbling along as quick as I could. I followed the hall to the front door.

The woman's purse was looped around the knob, the way she'd said it would be. I opened it, clawed through it. Found a brass circle loaded with keys.

I pushed the door open, peeked out. I saw a hall of doors, other apartments. There were two elevators right in the center of it. A red lightbulb shone above the door to the stairwell. I slipped out quickly and hurried toward it.

As I moved along the carpeted path, the doors to

two apartments opened. Eyes peered out at me, ghostly. No one spoke. I ignored them, moving as fast as I could, fingertips dragging along the brown wall.

I reached the red light. I hauled back on the heavy metal door, slid into the well. The moment I was inside, I heard the footsteps, rising to meet me.

I heard Watts's voice: "... enough backup to take over Long Island now."

And an answering growl: "Everyone saw him run for it."

"Asshole," said Watts. "Endangering innocent fucking people..."

On tiptoe, I climbed the stairs to the fifth landing. I waited there, crouched on the next step up, fighting against my heavy breathing. I heard the two cops stop on the landing below me.

"This is it," said Watts.

I peeked around the corner in time to see him go through the door. He was with Rankin now. Saint Francis might still be in Mrs. Hooterman's apartment, or he might be stationed outside.

I pulled back as Watts and Rankin went through the door, out of the stairwell.

Then I was moving again. Tumbling down the stairs, my feet dancing out in front of me. I was coughing as I passed the first floor. I continued on down to the basement level.

The stairs ended in a small cellar. A tight concrete space laced with shadows. A dull light spilled from a doorway around a corner. The laundry room probably. I could hear a washing machine chugging and gurgling. Right in front of me, a corridor twisted

away between concrete pillars. At the end of it, I saw
a set of wooden doors, padlocked together in the center.

I came away from the stairwell. I crept forward,
feeling for the smallest key on the brass ring. I wove
carefully between the pillars. Past them. To the
doors. I fit the woman's key to the padlock.

"Hello?"

I spun around. An old man stood at the entrance
to the laundry room. A flowered sheet dangled down
between his two hands. He was staring right at me.

I pressed back. The shadows streaked my face.
"It's just me," I said. "I have to go out for a minute."

The man looked at me unsurely. Then, unsurely,
he nodded. "Seeya later," he said.

"Right," I answered. I turned my back on him,
twisted the key. The padlock snapped open. I pushed
through the wooden doors, out into the alley and the
cool night.

The alley ran through the darkness toward Lexington
Avenue. It was a thin path cluttered with garbage,
dank with its smell. A streetlamp just beyond my
view sent a dull streak of light over the pavement. I
stood still a moment and let the key ring slip from
my hand. I heard the chink of it as it hit the ground.
Then I took a breath and followed the light toward
the street.

A horn blared as I came out from between the
buildings. I looked right, toward Eighty-sixth. The
glow of red flashers whirled over the corner building.
In the distance, more sirens bayed to each other like
wolves.

On the sidewalk across from me was the entrance

to the subway, the Lexington line. There were cabs cruising by me, heading downtown. I ran my hand over my mouth. It came away slick with sweat. It was hard to come down, hard to think. Impossible, it seemed like, to figure the angles.

But then, there was only one place I figured I would be safe. And the subway was the fastest way to get there. It was my best shot, the toughest to trace, the hardest to stop. After another second, I came out of the alley shadows. I made my move.

I jammed my hands into my pockets, ducked my head behind my jacket collar. I took long strides as I headed for the corner. It was hard to keep my legs going. They felt leaden and wobbly at the same time. The sirens got louder. The buildings on the far side of Eighty-sixth began to flash red, too. I got to the corner and saw the "Don't Walk" sign glaring at me from across the way. I started to jaywalk across.

Now the sirens were screaming. They were throbbing in my ears. With a sudden glare of twirling red, two cop cars broke through the intersection, raced across Eighty-sixth. They were past in a moment. I heard their sirens die away—as if they'd pulled to the curb right behind me and stopped. I didn't look back. I just kept walking.

A step. A step. Another step. I made it to the far side. My legs felt like they were ready to buckle. But now the stairs to the subway were right in front of me. I could see down into the entranceway. There was a short flight leading to a concrete landing, then more stairs around the corner going down into the station. I forced myself on, not looking left or right.

I was a yard away, a step away, I was reaching out for the banister with a shaking hand—when another siren started up, close by. Without pausing, I glanced around. I saw a cruiser a half-block north, speeding down toward me on Lexington.

Just then, my hand touched the cold subway banister. I yanked myself in. I went tripping down the stairs fast as I could. Touched the platform, spun around the corner fast.

A cop was coming up the next flight toward me.

He was a littly guy. Round-faced Italian with a heavy black mustache. I saw something flicker in his eyes as we headed toward each other. Something mechanical and coplike. I didn't miss a step as I skittered past him.

I hit bottom. The underground hall. Token booth ahead to my left. Turnstiles to my right, the train platform and the tracks just beyond them. I drove my legs toward the token booth. There was a line of three or four people there. As I came toward them, there was a low rumble. Then it broke into a sudden roar. A train shot into the station. About twenty people on the platform crowded toward it. The people at the token booth pressed closer together, buying their tokens as fast as they could. I kept moving toward them.

"Hey!"

It came from the stairs behind me. The cop's voice. I looked back. He wasn't in sight yet. He hadn't come back down.

But he called again: "Hey!"

I swerved from my course. Turned away from the

booth. Headed for the exit gates, reaching into my jacket for my wallet at the same time.

The train stopped. I heard its brakes squealing. The people on the platform gathered around the doors.

"This is the express train," the announcer said. "This is *not* the local train. This is the express, next stop Fifty-ninth Street."

I grabbed the exit gate, pulled it open. Held my wallet up above my head as if I were flashing identification. The subway's doors slid open.

From the corner of my eye, I saw the cop come down out of the stairway behind me. But he hesitated there, unsure he'd made his man.

"You there! Excuse me?" he called.

I was through the gate. I was heading along the platform to the train. Now the cop knew.

He shouted: "Hey! Hold it!"

The last passengers crowded onto the train. I flew in after them.

"Hey!"

The doors slid shut behind me. The train gave a jerk. It began to move.

I knew I should hide my face. I knew I shouldn't look back. But I couldn't help it. I raised my eyes to the window.

The cop had not reached the platform yet. He was standing at the exit gate, staring at me. He started to turn back to the booth.

The train rolled out of the station, into the dark.

Sweat poured off me now. My mouth hung open. My heartbeat seemed to be rocking everything inside me. I moved—I staggered—to a seat. Dropped into it. I leaned my head back, my eyes closed. I felt the jar and rhythm of the racing train.

After a moment, I thought of my scraped cheek, the blood drying on my hand. I was disheveled, conspicuous. I opened my eyes, looked around the car. No one seemed to pay me any mind. The train rattled through the long tunnel. The walls at the window were a blur of blackness. I passed my gaze from one passenger to the next. None of them looked back at me. A bearded young man, earphones in his ears, read a textbook, bobbing his head to music I couldn't hear. A husky black man stared at the *Star* wearily. A brown woman in nursing whites sat motionless in a corner, her hands folded in her lap, her eyes trained on an ad for Combat roach killer.

My gaze passed over each of them. My heart beat. The sweat rolled down my brow. But none of them seemed to notice me. None of them met my eyes. My gaze moved on to the storm door—the door that led out between this car and the next. I could see through its window and through the window of the car beyond. I could see the people in there, too. I could see them in their seats, hunched over their papers, holding up their books, staring at the ads posted above their heads.

And I could see a patrolman walking down the aisle between them, checking the face of everyone he passed as he came closer and closer and closer to my car.

22

The subway broke out of the tunnel, into the station at Seventy-seventh Street. It pounded past the waiting people without breaking stride. The billboards, the white tiles on the station walls, whipped by in a haze of color. We plunged quickly into the tunnel again.

The cop in the next car was halfway down the aisle now. He'd stopped for a second to rouse a drunk, get a look at him. He was a tall, chunky fellow, this cop. He didn't smile. He didn't look like he had ever smiled. I sat still as he came on again methodically. His steady progress made him seem inevitable.

Still, I worked my way to my feet. I turned my back on him and stumbled up the length of the car. There were other cars ahead. No cops in there. Maybe I could just stay away from the guy until the train reached Fifty-ninth. Maybe I could get off there, slip away.

Not very likely. I'd been spotted. The cop on the train wasn't the only one who'd been alerted. There were sure to be others—plenty of others—waiting for me when the train pulled in.

All the same, with a grunt, I yanked open the heavy storm door. I stepped out between the cars.

The wind of the tunnel washed over me. The couplings jolted this way and that beneath my feet. The train wheels rumbled. The tracks spat sparks. The guard chains swung dizzily to and fro. Beyond them, there was a little gate, but it didn't do much. If you went past those chains, there was plenty of room to fall to the tracks.

To steady myself, I reached out and grabbed the handle of the next door over. I let go of the door behind me and it slid shut. I braced myself to push into the car ahead. Then I stopped. As I looked into the car through the window, I saw two more cops enter it from the far side.

They were an unpleasant pair. A fat one and a skinny one, both with hot, heavy-browed eyes. Their mouths were thin and wicked. They kept their hands to their holsters as they started down the aisle. One by one, they checked the faces of the passengers. Coming toward me just as steadily as the guy behind me was.

As I watched them, frozen, the train took a hard turn. My knees bent, my foot slipped. I clung hard to the door handle with both hands to keep from flying out into the racing blackness. I had to get off the couplings, back inside. But as I glanced over my shoulder I saw that the first cop was now coming into the car I'd just left. I was caught. An android linebacker behind me. Ahead of me, Laurel and Hardy from Hell.

The steady roar of the tunnel became a sudden

loud, rattling crash as we coursed out into the Sixty-eighth Street station. The station lights flashed at me between the cars, making me wince. The train seemed to speed up. It rocked back and forth hard. I was jarred to the side. The door handle slipped from my grasp.

I tumbled to the right, across the couplings, into the chains. I gasped. Grabbed hold of them, reached desperately for the car to steady myself. Now, as I held on, I could see Patrolmen Fat and Skinny through the window. They were almost to the end of the aisle. They were maybe twenty seconds from coming out the door, out to where I was.

I let go of the car wall, grabbed the swaying chains with both hands. I crouched down and began to ease my legs out underneath them. As they went out—out into the nothing, out into the speed and the noise and the nothing—I turned over, still gripping that chain. The links burned my palm. My muscles ached, weary, loosening. I lowered my legs down behind me, feeling with my feet for something—anything—other than that screaming, empty air.

I slipped. My knee slipped over the edge. I cried out, waiting for the onrushing wall to crush me. Then there was something... The toe of my right foot hit it. Some handle there, something for workmen to stand on. I got my right foot onto it, then my left. I slid my hands down the chain as far as I could. I lowered myself the rest of the way over the edge of the couplings.

And I hung there. I felt the walls of the tunnel tearing by my back. The rumble of the wheels surrounded me. Sparks shot up from the tracks around my feet. Above me, I heard the car door crash open.

Out came Fat and Skinny, passing from one car to the next. They could have seen me. Easily. They could have looked to one side and seen my head and shoulders above the couplings. My goodness, they could have said to one another, there is an idiot with his ass hanging over speeding death. But neither of these officers of the law was so stupid as to stay out between two subway cars any longer than he had to. Fat opened one door even as Skinny closed the other. They passed from car to car without turning toward me. They went in to meet their colleague and trade the report that I had not been found.

I cried out, startled. The tunnel had opened again and now the brakes were screaming. The noise drilled into me. I gritted my teeth against it, clinging to the chain as the subway slowed. We had reached the Fifty-ninth Street station.

The platform was on the far side of me. I could see it through the space between the cars. I had a glimpse of a small cluster of blue uniforms out there. Then we'd gone past them. The brakes squealed again. The train stopped.

I could barely open my hands. They wouldn't let the chain go. When they did, I clawed at the coupling, dragging myself back up onto the train. I stood up, pressed back, away from the station platform, close to the door. I peeked out through the train's window and saw the three cops exiting with the other passengers. They walked back along the platform. I saw them through the train windows. They joined the cluster of other cops. They all spoke together.

As they did, the doors of the train slid closed again. The body of the machine punched forward. I fell back against the chain, my heel going over the edge of the couplings. With a curse, I reached for the door handle, grasped it. I pulled the door open and tumbled into the car.

A few passengers glanced up as I stumbled forward gasping. A few. Then they looked at their papers, at their books, at their ads again. I moved to the corner seat, the nearest one. I fell into it.

My jaw hung slack, my eyes stared at nothing. The train carried me downtown to my destination.

23

"Wells!"

Lansing caught me as I fell through her door.

"I ran . . ."

"What are you doing here?"

"I ran away."

"The cops are looking—"

"I ran away from the cops, Lansing."

"What?"

"I ran away."

"Oh Jesus. What did you do?"

I could barely stand. My legs had finally given. She had me by the arm and I swayed in her grasp. Tears of exhaustion were pouring down my cheeks. They ran into the open wounds there. The salt stung.

Lansing got a better hold on me, grabbed me around the waist. I flung my arm over her shoulder, trying not to fall.

"Lance!" I kept gasping at her, trying to speak.

"Shut up, Wells. Be quiet."

We stumbled together toward a cushioned chair. I tumbled down toward it, taking her with me. My body went slack against the cushions. I tried to hold her, talk to her again as she disentangled herself and stood. Instead, I started coughing. A damp cough from deep in my lungs. The phlegm boiled up into my throat. I leaned back, swallowing hard, gasping for air.

Lansing was on her knees next to me. She held my arm in her two hands. She pressed her face against my shoulder.

"What did you do?" she repeated softly.

"He'll kill me, Lancer. He's gonna kill me. . . . " The coughing started up again. It was a long moment before I could force it back. "Oh God," I muttered. "Oh shit. Oh God."

Without thinking, I reached into my shirt pocket, brought out my cigarettes.

"God," I whispered.

"What are you . . . ?"

I fumbled a butt from the pack.

"Wells, you can't . . ."

"God . . ."

"Stop." I didn't listen to her. "Stop, please," she said. I brought out the cigarette. Suddenly, she started to scream: "Stop it! Stop it, what are you, stop, stop!" She slapped wildly at my hands. The pack flew out of them. Cigarettes scattered in the air as the pack spiraled to the rug.

I turned my head to look at her. She was staring at my hands, my shaking hands. Her eyes burned bright and crazy. She wrapped her fingers around my palm, lowered her face to my leg, and started to cry.

I sat still, breathing hard. I felt her tears coming through my pants leg. I felt her trembling. In the quiet apartment—the garden side of a SoHo brown-

stone—I heard classical music playing softly somewhere. I heard her sob.

I moved my free hand to touch her hair. I passed
my fingers through it. The long gold strands were
silken to the touch. My hand went over them again
and again, then shifted to her cheek. I felt the
dampness on her skin. Then she turned and I felt her
lips. She kissed my palm gently.

"Why did you do it?" she said through the tears.
"Why did you do it, John?"

I shook my head. "I don't know. Christ. I had him.
I had him dead to rights, and now he's after me."

She came off my leg. Turned to me, her hair
fanning out behind her, her eyes going hot.

"Is that all? Is that all?"

I looked at her a long time. Her cameo face, her
blue eyes swimming. Her porcelain skin pink and
mottled with tears.

My voice was thick. "I'm scared, Lansing. He's a
cop, for Christ's sake. He's a cop and he's after me,
he's trying to kill me, he's trying to . . ."

She came to me. Climbed onto me. Put her cool
hands on the sides of my face, pressed her lips
against my forehead.

"A man is dead," I whispered. "Someone has to
pay."

"He attacked you."

"I don't know what happened anymore."

"He tried to kill you. You fought back."

"And now they're after me."

"It's all right. It's going to be all right."

"Christ, Christ, Christ, Lansing. What're they gonna

do? They gonna arrest me? I mean, is that it? They're gonna put me on trial for murder? I mean, Christ, Lansing! I mean, Jesus Christ!" I wrapped my arms around her. I pressed my hands into her back, felt her breasts against me. "What the hell happened here? What the hell is going on? I had him."

We sat that way a long time. A long time while I stared over her shoulder into the bright room. Colors. There were lots of colors everywhere and lots of curves. The walls peach, peach arches over the doorways to the kitchen and the hall. Tapestries on the walls, dark red, bright gold. The rugs—lots of small rugs over the floor—deep blue, electric yellow. And funny old furniture—old sewing chairs, giant pillows, an inlaid coffee table—crowded together in the small space and all of it pink and paisley and deep brown.

Lansing had her cheek against my cheek. Then she turned her head to lay her lips there. I kept staring past her into the room.

"There's got to be an answer," I said.

I felt her lips part. I felt them move away from me. She sat up on my lap, looked down at me.

"What are you going to do?"

"I've got to think."

"Wells. Wells, you've gotta go in."

I glanced at her, but couldn't meet her eyes. I shifted out from under her, letting her down onto the chair. I stood up and took a pace away.

"You've gotta go in," she said. "You're giving them everything they need to convict you."

"I've gotta think, Lansing, I've gotta . . ."

"Wells."

I spun to her, my fist clenched, the anger flaring in me. "There's gotta be an answer here."

She stood. She stepped close to me, eyes on mine. "He's the law, Wells."

"Not my law, not him."

"He's a cop."

"He's a mob killer with a fucking badge. I had that. I had that solid."

"Wells!" She barked it at me, but then her voice went quiet: "Listen to me. Listen to me, okay? You've got to let it go. You had him, I know, but things have changed."

"I still can get him."

"We'll bring in a lawyer..."

"Oh yeah, fucking F. Lee Bailey, I'll do fucking life with that guy..."

"Would you listen?"

"I'm telling you, Lance..."

"Just listen, John, listen. We'll get a lawyer, a different lawyer, a good one. We'll go in—"

"I gotta think."

"You turn yourself in. You get out on bail..."

"They're charging me with murder. I tried to escape, they won't give me bail. Once he gets me in there..."

"We will get you out, John. Once you're out, we'll go after this. Okay? We can—"

"Listen, Lance. Listen. Would you just listen to me?"

"Wells, please. This is crazy."

I stepped to her. I put my hands on her face. I gazed down at her. Her eyes were filling again.

"Listen," I said. "There's an answer here. I'm close to it. I followed your leads."

"What leads, what do you . . . ?"

"The house, Cooper House, Baumgarten . . ."

"We'll cover all that."

"There's a woman, too. She's dead. An overdose."

"What? I don't . . ." Her lips trembled, as if she might cry again.

"Ssh," I said. "Listen."

"I don't understand. I don't understand what you're talking about. What woman?"

"Just a woman at Cooper House, the bookkeeper."

"The bookkeeper."

"Mikki Snow, her name was. She was onto something . . ."

"Wells, I don't—"

"Something about Howard Baumgarten."

"I don't get this. The comptroller?"

"She went to him—I don't know why—then she quit—now they've found her, see? You see what I'm saying?"

"*No!* A bookkeeper? What . . . ?" She lowered her face. A tear fell onto the rug. A darkened spot between two white cigarettes lying there.

"Maybe she killed herself," I said. "It could mean something. I just have to . . ."

"I don't get it. I don't see. What does this have to do with you?"

I let her go. I left her standing there, crying. I paced away from her. I turned, paced toward her. She was fighting off the tears now. Wiping her face with her hand, running the hand up through her hair to straighten it.

"I don't know," I said. "That's the thing. That's the key to it."

"You just can't do this," Lansing said.

I paced. "There's got to be some link between what Snow found and me."

"We can protect you from Watts."

"I mean, some reason why I figured into it." I paced toward her.

"You're making yourself look guilty."

I paced away. "That story I wrote, that old story..."

"They'll put you away."

I paced toward her. I fought her voice. "They would have read that at Cooper House, seen my byline."

"They'll put you away and you're not guilty."

I paced away. "But so what? It was just straight news." I paced toward her.

"You're not guilty for killing Reich. You're not guilty for any of it. For losing Watts, any of it. You've got to stop doing this. You're not guilty, you're not guilty—"

I grabbed the front of her blouse. "Shut up!"

"No!"

"Shut up!" I shook her. There were tears in my eyes. "I killed him!"

"I don't care."

"Why don't you ever shut up?"

"Because I love you!" She grabbed my hands, digging her nails into them. "Because I love you and you're innocent. You understand? You're innocent, whether you like it or not."

I yanked her to me, kissed her. I held her hard as her hands dug into my hair, her nails sharp. I wanted to be in her. My Lansing. I was half-blind with the hunger for her.

She started crying again as I brought her down to the floor. Crying with her arms flung out, hands grabbing at the rug, fists clenching it. Her head rocked back and forth. I stared at her face, stared and stared at it. My hand was up under her skirt. I clutched at her panty hose, tore it away.

She screamed once as I came into her. She clawed at my shirt, trying to touch me, trying to get at the flesh, getting at it. I pulled her blouse open, ran my hands over her. I said her name over and over. I stared and stared at her. She was so beautiful. I came into her and into her. She was so warm.

24

I woke up suddenly.

"What time . . . ?"

"Ten. Just after ten."

I nodded. I groaned as I sat up. My back was tied in a knot. My neck had turned to stone. My legs ached, my lungs ached. And where the pain couldn't find a place a settle, it just spread out, became a general throb.

I looked around. I'd been lying on the floor. The big pillows had been arranged around me as a make-shift bed. One of those fancy, handmade country quilts had been thrown over me.

Lansing was across the room. She was sitting on a window seat, her back against the wall, her knees drawn up. She had a mug of coffee balanced on her knees. She'd turned most of the lights out, but there was one small lamp on a table by her, glowing. I could see her in her blue bathrobe, her legs white, bare to the thigh.

"You ruined my clothes, John," she whispered.

"You ruined my flesh, Angela. You can buy new clothes."

"I'm a reporter, dearest."

"So you can buy old clothes. What am I going to do about my body?"

"That's the question all New York is asking. You were on the radio half an hour ago."

"My old recording of 'Stardust'?"

"Not exactly."

"They never get tired of the standards. Mark my word. The pendulum will swing back."

She laughed. "You sound kind of chipper over there, old man."

"I do that just before I die. It's a bad habit."

But I smiled at her. I did feel fairly decent, at that. There had been a moment's peace inside her. It was good. It lingered.

I looked away. Started lifting up the pillows, searching under them.

"On the coffee table," Lansing said.

I saw the cigarettes there, clustered around the crumpled pack, near an ashtray. I threw the quilt aside, got up, padded over to them. I was naked now, and I could feel Lansing's eyes on me. I picked a cigarette off the table, stuck it in my mouth.

"Stop looking at me like that, Lansing," I said.

"You have the worst physique of any human being I've ever seen in my entire life."

"I'm really just a dead body animated by the spirit of revenge."

"Do you exercise to get like that?"

"Where are my matches?" I patted my chest. "Where are my pockets?"

"Over on the floor, by the pillows. Take the ashtray. What is that, on your shoulder?"

I returned to my pallet, ashtray in hand. "That woman. In the woods. When I was but a child your age. Hell, I've told you that story."

"Oh yeah, the sharpened stake. Boy, it's wicked-looking, isn't it?"

"Ayuh." I held on to my back as I settled onto the floor again. "Jesus," I said. I found my matches, lit my cigarette, and leaned back, groaning a mouthful of smoke. "So what are they saying about me? On the radio, I mean."

Lansing glanced out the window, sipped her coffee. "It isn't good."

"Are they playing it big?"

"Hell, yes. It's a good story. I'd play it big, too."

"Great. I hope we're off-the-record here."

"Deep off, big guy."

"So come on, what'd they say, Lansing?"

"You know, I liked it when you called me Angela."

"Why? Is that your name?"

She laughed again.

"What a guess," I said. "Now what the hell did they say?"

"They had a woman on."

"Uh oh. Old woman? Mrs. Hooterman?"

"No, she wasn't old. Joanne Ryan. She said the police were firing at you. Indiscriminately, that was the word she used. Through her window, too. I mean, Jesus. Did they?"

"Oh yeah."

"She said they almost killed her son. That you rescued him."

"Okay. So that's good, right?"

"No, not so good. Watts had to come back with something. And he did, in spades. He made you sound like a very bad man, Mr. Wells. He said the police had reason to fear for the woman's life, for her kid . . . all that shit."

"He's gotta do that. He's gotta go all the way. Either he's right about Reich, or I'm right about E. J. McMahon. If he doesn't go all the way, he's finished."

"So it's your word against his," said Lansing. "And his word is that you are one very dangerous desperado."

I smoked quietly a second. Feeling the safety of the apartment around me, feeling the big, dark and dangerous city beyond. Finally, I looked over at Lansing. Watched her sitting and sipping her coffee, framed against the night. "How come you're all the way over there?" I said, "Are you, like, a lookout?"

"They'll check this place out soon, you know."

"Well, they won't come through the garden. Come here."

"What for?"

"Just come here," I said.

She put the mug aside, slid down from the window seat, trying not to smile. She strolled to me slowly, lowered herself to my side. I took a few long breaths, looking her over. Then I tugged her bathrobe open. I laid my hand on her waist. I leaned toward her, kissed her. She pressed to me, too, our tongues together.

When she pulled back, she studied me. "Uh oh," she said. "You're getting that look."

"What look?"

"That look you get. Like: What've I done, she's just a child. Like it's wrong, like you're sorry. I hate that look."

"I can't help it. You need a man with a bright future—or just with a future."

She stroked my face. "Don't say that, okay?"

"Why not?"

"'Cause I happen to be scared out of my wits."

"How come? Morgenstern's not your lawyer."

Her eyes brightened slightly. "Does that mean you'll turn yourself in?"

"I don't know." I took her hand. I played with the fingers. "I didn't mean to do this to you."

"Oh, it felt like you did."

"Not that, dimwit. To come here. To make you an accessory. I didn't mean to do that. I didn't know where else to go."

"I'm glad," she said. "I'm glad this is where you came."

I shook my head. "Damn it. I just keep thinking: If Mikki Snow were still alive. You know? If I could talk to her. Maybe then I'd stand a chance."

Lansing looked at me. Brushed my hair back with her free hand. I chewed on her fingertip thoughtfully.

"John," she whispered.

"If there was ever a connection between Thad Reich and me, she must've been the one who..." I stopped.

"What?"

I turned Lansing's hand over in my own. "Maybe that's the whole thing."

"What thing?"

"I mean, maybe that was the connection."

"Wells. What connection?"

"I don't know. I'm not sure. It's the timing of it that's off. She went to see Baumgarten... And then when I ask him about it, Herd shows up..."

"John, this is driving me crazy—would you tell me what you're talking about?"

"And those books," I said.

I let Lansing go. I sat up, away from her. I jabbed my cigarette out in the tray.

"Damn it, what?" she said.

"I need your car."

"Oh no."

I got up, groped for my clothes.

"Absolutely not, John."

I pulled on my underwear, my pants. I reached for my shirt.

"Damn it, John!"

"I'm taking your car, kid."

"Then I'm coming with you."

"No, you're not."

She jumped to her feet, belting her robe furiously. "Yes, I am."

"This isn't a discussion." I pulled on my shirt. Worked the buttons. "There are cops after me. They have guns."

"They won't shoot me."

"Right. 'Cause you'll be here."

"I am coming with you, Wells."

"Lansing, if I have to knock you out, so help me I will."

"Oh, you will not."

"Well, maybe not, but the thought is there. Gimme the keys."

"Oh!" Her face flushed. She stomped away from me, two steps. Then she spun back. "Goddamn it. Are you always this infuriating?"

"Uh..."

She folded her arms beneath her breasts. Her eyes filled. I was on the floor again, pulling on my socks, my shoes. I stood up.

"Where are the keys?" She glared at me. "Where are the keys, Lansing?"

"In my purse, on the door."

I went to the door. Rummaged through the purse. "Seems like I just did this. Last time, the woman had tried to stab me to death."

"Yeah, well, the night's young, pal." She did not sound like she was kidding.

I had the keys. I was pulling my jacket on now. Lansing watched me, her lips set.

"If you expect me to stand at the door and breathlessly tell you to be careful, forget it."

I went to the door. "I'll be back, Lansing."

She came after me. I took hold of her, pressed her against me.

"I'm going into the office," she said. "I'm going to monitor the scanner. I'm going to get on the phone with Gottlieb, with anyone who'll talk to me, anyone I can. I'll keep track of them—and if you need help, if you need to know where they are, what they're up to..."

"I'll call in."

"Call in," she said.

"I will."

"Wells . . ." She looked up at me.

I kissed her. We kissed for a long time. When we broke apart, I held her and gazed at her face again, trying to take it all in, trying to hold on to it. "Thanks, Lansing."

"That's not what I want to hear, Wells."

"I'll be back," I said again.

And I left her.

25

Lansing had her little hatchback parked on the street half a block away. I hurried to it, over the tree-lined sidewalk. I huddled behind my collar as I walked, but only a young couple passed, and they took no notice of me.

I slipped into the car—a red Honda Accord. It felt good—it felt safe—to close the door, to start it up, to start moving. To get away.

I headed for West Street, nice and easy, obeying the traffic laws like a saint. Soon, I was on the highway. Speeding up, the soft wind at the window. Heading north beside the Hudson, the Jersey lights beaming over the water to my left. When I crossed the Harlem River, the relief burst over me. To be traveling on the dark, swift roads. To be off the island of Manhattan. It felt very, very good.

I didn't remember Baumgarten's address, the home address Ray had given me. But I remembered the street name in the town of Bedford. I thought that would be enough. I headed there.

It was about 11:30 when I cruised into the quaint town square. Main Street was dead. The restored white clapboard shops on it stared with black windows across the sward of grass that was once the common. On a little hill rising from the common's other side, antique graves slanted this way and that, pale white beneath the black and swaying trees.

I rolled past this, around a bend in the road. Under the shadow of a high rock. A few dozen more yards and a small intersection appeared to my left. It was almost hidden by shrubbery. Mountain Road. That was the name of it. A gravel path rising steeply, up toward the top of the rock. I turned the Honda onto it. I bounded over the gravel, straining at the climb.

I was almost at the summit when I saw Baumgarten's name on a mailbox at the side of the road. I turned into a rocky dirt driveway flanked by hedges. I came through them into a wide, open yard. It was big, more than an acre, the big sky with its half-moon bright above it. There were shadows of trees—oaks and willows—against the sky. And the shadow of a house, a big hulking house with two fresh wings and several dormers in the peaked roof. There was a light on in one of the dormer windows. The house lights— the outside lights—were off.

I killed my own headlights. Rolled up the driveway slowly. There was a Lincoln parked outside the garage. I pulled in behind it. When I stopped the engine, I could hear the quiet all around me. Then, in the quiet, I could hear crickets and cicadas, birds and frogs chattering in the trees and the grass.

I stepped out of the car. The nervousness—the fear—worked in my stomach like a slow, steady machine. That moment of peace—that moment of Lansing: even the last of it had drifted away.

I walked up the front path to the door, a door with a curtained window. I rang the bell. Heard the old-fashioned ding-dong. I stood and waited, rubbing my hands together.

I rang again. There was a second's pause, then a light flashed on behind the door's window. After another second, a porch light on the wall above my head flashed on too. The window curtains parted. Howard Baumgarten's eagle face peered out at me and frowned.

The knob turned hard. He yanked the door open. His bald head rippled down over his deep eyes. His big body blocked the entrance.

"What do you want?"

"It's a money laundry, isn't it? Cooper House. You pass your kickbacks through it as donations. That's why the feds couldn't get you. They couldn't find the cash."

It was hard to tell in the dim light, but he seemed to go pale. He didn't move, though. He stood his ground, solid.

"I'm going to call the cops now, Wells," he said. "If I were you, I'd run for my life."

He started to shut the door. I stuck my foot in the opening. He closed the door on it hard.

"Agh! Shit," I said.

He leaned on the door. I hit it with my shoulder, caught him off balance. He fell back a few steps into the house. I pushed in after him.

I came into a small foyer. A stairway led up from it

into darkness. Under the stairway there was a small table with a phone on it. Baumgarten went for it, picked up the receiver.

"The books before the Board of Estimate vote are practically empty. After it, they're full up, too full. Those are your people, aren't they?" I said. "Kicking back their salaries for jobs. You agreed to win over the board if Cooper would give you a place to hide the cash."

Baumgarten snorted. Looked over his shoulder at me. "You haven't got that. You haven't got a thing." He started to dial.

I wiped the sweat from my face with the back of my hand.

"Maybe not," I said. "But I know where to look."

"Hello, Sergeant," Baumgarten said into the phone. "This is Howard Baumgarten on Mountain Road. John Wells, the reporter being hunted by the New York City police, has just forced his way into my house."

I lit a cigarette, dropped the match on the rug.

"He's standing right here, making threats at me," Baumgarten said. Then he said: "Thank you. I'll be waiting."

He hung up. He turned to me. He smiled thinly. "You want a cup of coffee? Or would you rather have a head start?"

"I'll stay," I said. "I'd rather have the Westchester guys take me than the NYPD anyway."

"Good. Then everyone's happy."

"And when they do take me, and when the papers interview me, and when they put me on trial, I'm gonna tell them what I think. I'm gonna tell them that the money is on Cooper's books. It leaves a trail, Howard. It always does. And once the feds and the press and the city start looking in the right places, they'll run it down and track it right back to you."

I could see him clearly now in the foyer. He was pale, all right. Still, his mouth was set, his eyes hard. "You can't prove any of it," he said roughly.

"I don't have to. I just have to start it off. How much will it take? A story about the money laundry. A piece on Mikki Snow. And then a little investigative work into her death."

His hard eyes softened. He swallowed, licked his lips. "What's that supposed to mean?"

"You know damn well what it means. You're hooked in everywhere."

He was breathing hard now. "So if I talk to you, you'll burn me anyway."

"Probably."

"So what's the difference?"

"About fifteen years, if you go down for Snow. And you could. Why not? She came to you first."

He wiped his mouth with his palm. "Listen, Wells, you know that's bullshit..."

"And you know I didn't murder Thad Reich."

"I have a wife, Wells. I have children. I have a grandchild. I bought her a doll, for Christ's sake!"

"Why did Snow come to you? She want a piece of the action?"

He turned away. In the distance, down below the mountainside: that old siren song, just audible, growing louder.

Baumgarten glanced at the door. "They're coming. There's no time."

"Talk fast, then. Start now."

He glanced at the door again. Stalling maybe. Maybe trying to think. "Snow thought... She thought I... She wanted me to stop... To stop passing the money through. She was... She thought I'd forced it on her."

"On Cooper."

"Yeah, yeah. She wanted me to take the pressure off Cooper, she said, or she'd... tell the feds."

The siren grew louder. It was still on the road below us, though. I fought to keep my breathing steady.

A woman's voice drifted down to us from the shadows at the top of the stairs.

"Howard? Is everything all right down there?"

"Yes, everything's fine, dear. I'm just—"

"Come on, damn it," I whispered.

"Everything's fine. It's just a friend."

"All right," the woman said. "Come up soon, though. It's getting late."

"All right, I will."

The volume of the siren went up a notch.

"Come on," I said again. "So she was trying to save Cooper. Trying to keep her out of trouble."

Baumgarten scratched his bald head. "I don't know. I don't know what she wanted. I kept telling her, I told her: it was Cooper's idea. She came to me, made the offer to me. She didn't have the money to go up against Sturgeon, so she asked me. I mean, she's a savvy broad. I was doing her a *favor*, for Christ's

sake." He lifted one hand. "Snow didn't believe me.
I told her, I said, 'Go ask her. You don't believe me?
Ask her,' I said. I said—"

All at once, the siren seemed to break up and out
into the night around us. The cop car had turned the
corner onto Mountain Road. It was climbing toward
Baumgarten's house, coming steadily over the rough
terrain. I started panting to the quick rhythm of my
heart.

Baumgarten's eyes went back to the door. His
mouth trembled. The sweat around it glistened. "I
called Celia. I told her what'd happened. She said
she'd take care of it. Mikki loved her, she said. I
figured there was no . . . Wells, for the love of God,
you'll ruin my whole fucking family."

The words burst from him just as the red flashers
appeared. As they passed over the dark and lit the
trees outside. The siren blooped off. The cruiser was
coming up the last stretch of Mountain Road. Its
lights passed over the hedges.

"Why did you call Mark Herd?" I hissed at him.
My teeth started knocking together. "When you came
to see me, why did you call Mark Herd?"

Outside, I could hear the cop car slow. I looked
over my shoulder. Saw the top of its flasher above the
hedge that flanked the driveway.

Baumgarten stared at me crazily. "Run!" he
whispered. "Run!"

"It's too late for that."

"Please."

"Why'd you call him?"

"Not Herd. Cooper. You can still get out of here. You can go. Go."

He pointed at the door behind me. I heard the first rustle of gravel as the cop car began its turn into the drive. For another instant, I fought the urge to break for it. Then I heard the gravel crunch as the cruiser started toward the house.

"Run!" said Baumgarten again.

And I did.

26

I bolted without thinking. I bolted for the door. Banged through it, out into the night. The police car was just starting down the long drive, heading forward to park behind Lansing's Honda. The headlights were inching up toward me. I ran straight for them.

I ran to the little car. Crouched down, hoping to keep the shadows over me, hoping to beat the lights. The breath broke out of my lungs as I slammed into the Honda's side. I grabbed hold of the door handle, pulled it back.

The coppers' headlights hit me. The flasher blinded me as its red light whirled over my face. I tumbled out of the glare, into the darkness of the car. I had the keys out of my pocket somehow. I pulled the door shut, fumbling desperately to find the ignition slot. The key kept slipping over the surface of the dash. It wouldn't go in. The lights grew close behind me.

Then the bullhorn thundered. "Step out of the car! Step out of the car!"

The key slid in. I turned it over. The engine gave a dull clunk, then growled and spun.

"Step out of the car now! Step out of the car right now!"

My rear window was all light. White light. Whirling red light. It flashed in my rearview. I had to squint it off.

Keeping my car dark, I threw it into forward. Baumgarten's Lincoln was a foot or two ahead of me. The cop car had moved up quick, locked me in behind. I wrenched the wheel over and hit the gas.

The compact swung around, breathing by the Lincoln's rear fender. I bumped off the driveway, onto the lawn. I careened across the grass, still turning, turning around.

I saw the cops emerging from their car. I saw the black shadows of them in the whirling light. One on the far side, one near me. I saw them stepping to the side going for their holsters. I nudged the brake as the Honda kept spinning around over the grass. Now the lights were at my side window. Now they burned into me through the windshield. Now, through the windshield, I saw the two cops lifting their revolvers, leveling them steady in their clasped hands.

I straightened the wheel out and hit the gas. I sped toward the cruiser, rocking over the broken ground.

For one second, I saw the cop on the near side clearly. His clean-cut, young, and earnest face. His terrified blue eyes. I saw him try to keep his gun steady. Then he cried out and jumped out of the Honda's way, rolling back across the hood of the cruiser. At the same instant, I threw the wheel over. The left tires lifted off the ground as the Accord swerved to avoid the cops. Again, I hit the gas, shot down the driveway, aimed for the opening between the hedges.

And the other cop, the one on the far side of the car, opened fire.

Glass crunched and shattered. I didn't know where. Somewhere on the Accord I heard the sound as the bullet slammed into it. In the wild scarlet light from the cruiser, I saw the hedges rolling closer and closer to me. I pressed the gas petal as far down as it would go. The car bucked and punched out like a fist.

The cop fired again and I heard a whine and a hollow thud as a bullet buried itself in the car's metal. Then I was through the hedges, turning and turning on the rough road, gravel and dust spitting out behind me. I swerved until I was headed down the mountain—and then kept swerving, further and further around.

I hit the brakes. Wrestled with the wheel. Hit the gas again. With a lurch, the little car began rolling forward. Down the Mountain Road, down from the rock.

I turned the lights on then. I saw the road. It appeared to be falling away below me. I followed it, fast as I could.

27

By the time the cops came after me—by the time I heard their sirens start up again—I was off the rock and around the corner, heading away from the center of town. I saw a river wind out of the trees to my right. It ran past a house, tumbled over a waterfall. A dirt path opened on that side and followed the drop. I swung the Honda onto it, plunged down. Suddenly there was forest on every side. And darkness.

I pulled the Accord over to the shoulder—more of a ditch than a shoulder. I killed the lights, the engine. I sat there and listened. The crickets, the frogs, the forest noises rose up loudly out of the trees. Above that, I could still hear the siren. But only barely. It was fading away. The cops had headed off in the other direction. I'd lost them, for a while.

I glanced into the back seat, assessed the damage. A bullet had shattered one of the rear windows. The glass shards dangled from the frame, sparkled on the black seat cover. There was a jagged wound in the cover, too—a bullet hole. The yellow stuffing peeked out of it.

I took my shoe off, reached back, and cleared the shards from the window frame to make the break

look less conspicuous. I wondered where the other
bullet had gone. I wondered what Lansing would say
when she got a load of what I'd done to her car. I
could imagine her face when she saw it. It would be
like something out of a comic book, all sweat and
gritted teeth and rolling eyes. Luckily, there was a
good chance the cops would kill me before I had to
deal with her.

I lit a cigarette, took a long drag. Started the car
again, and rolled off slowly along the rough dirt of
the forest road. Now I had to make a plan, figure the
odds for getting away with it. Offhand, I figured the
odds were lousy.

I didn't think the cops had made my plates. Not
with my lights off, not in that chaos. But they had
the color and make of the car, that was certain. They
might even trace it to Lansing if they put their heads
together with NYPD. If I gave them time, anyway,
they'd be able to spot me coming for miles.

I didn't plan to give them time.

I drove on. There were no lights burning anywhere. What houses there were, set in behind the
trees, were just black shapes, hulking. For the most
part, the woods went back and back without a break.
Soon, though, the dirt road gave way to pavement.
Lawns appeared between patches of forest. The road
opened up a little. I started to pick up some speed.

I seemed to be heading east. I thought I might
pick my way through the back roads to Connecticut.
Take a crack at the Merritt Parkway or maybe travel
down on 124. The cops didn't have the manpower to
cover me everywhere. They'd have to guess or spot

me by chance. So far, it looked like I was outguessing them. I drove for a long time. Got onto the parkway, headed down toward the border. My luck held.

I smoked steadily as I drove. I smoked and watched the road and watched the mirror, looking for cops. I might have had a chance with them now, might have been able to explain, even prove my case. But it wasn't good enough, not with Watts after me. One night in jail might be fatal. A week on Rikers Island, I was dead for sure. I had to get one last answer. Then, if I could reach the *Star*, if I could convince the People Upstairs of the truth, if I could surrender to the cops with an army of lawyers surrounding me—then I just might be able to keep myself alive.

It was possible. It seemed possible, at least. But with every minute, the percentages shifted a little further against me. The more I traveled, the more chance there was some quick-eyed cop would nail my car. The more time went by, the likelier I'd make a mistake. As I rolled down into New York again, as the low cities of Westchester grew up along the road and as the night traffic grew thicker at the edge of the Bronx, my nerves began to heat up again. My eyes would not stay still. They flicked from the mirror to the pavement to the shoulders where the cops hide sometimes. I kept waiting for the sound of the siren, the whirl of the lights.

It did not happen, though, until after I hit the FDR. I shouldn't have gone that way, but I decided to risk a fast trip downtown and brave the heavier patrols. I stuck to the center lane, traveled just a little above the speed limit. By now, I was gripping the steering wheel so hard my knuckles were white. I didn't even dare to glance behind me anymore, afraid of what I'd see. The colored lights of Queens sparkled on the East River. The East River flashed by...

And then the lights burst over my rear window. The siren gave a whoop. I looked up to see the cruiser bearing down on me at full speed.

I hit the gas. The Accord lurched forward. The cop car had already pulled into the left lane. In another second, it was right beside me.

In a second more, it had sped past. Its siren screaming, its lights whirling round, it headed south on the FDR, until it rounded a bend and vanished from sight.

I eased my foot down on the brake. I eased my body back against the seat. The pulse in my throat almost choked me. I swallowed it. I drove on, to the exit at Forty-second Street.

There was no place to park near River City. I didn't have time to look around. I drove straight to Cooper House and stopped the Accord right out in front, blocking a fireplug.

I stepped outside. The night was cool and pleasant. The air was soft and spring sweet. There was traffic enough down on the avenue, but up and down the hill, everything was quiet. Only a bum, at the top of the road, shuffled through the sewer steam, heading toward the local park. I left the car behind me, crossed the street. Approached the towering limestone castle for the last time.

The front doors were closed. The heavy wood,

laced with iron, looked impregnable. The two windows to the drop-in center were within reach, though. They were shut, but I didn't think they were rigged with an alarm. There was a security guard inside, after all. He was the one to take care of break-ins.

I moved underneath the windows. They were about six feet off the ground. I could get my hands on them, my fingers on the glass. I gave one of them a push upward. I got nowhere, it was locked. I moved to the second, shoved up against the glass. It budged. I got under the sill and pushed it up as far as I could reach, about halfway.

I grabbed hold of the ledge. I tried to haul myself up. A sword of pain went through me. I gave a short cry, fell back to the pavement. My back: it had been wrung like a damp rag. I reached around to feel it, trying to catch my breath, coughing. Slowly, the pain eased to a dull throb.

With a low grunt, I stepped forward to try the window again.

Once more, I grabbed the ledge. I hauled up. Every muscle in my body was stretched and weary, coursing with fire. My jaw hurt—from when I'd slapped into that wall earlier. And my back now went ominously numb. I dragged myself up until I could throw an elbow over the ledge. I grabbed the window frame. Tried to bring my knee up. It slipped off, and the pain of the stone chipping my knee nearly made me fall again.

The next try did it. I got my knees up, balanced precariously on the ledge. I caught hold of the half-open window and shoved it up the rest of the

way. There was a screen beyond it. I tested it—
pushed at its frame gently.

The thing just gave way. It fell right into the room.
The edge of the frame hit the floor with a thud. The
screen toppled over, banging once against a chair
before it landed.

I followed the frame into the room. The second I
touched down, I heard the footsteps running toward
me from the hall. I dove to the floor. Scrambled
behind an easy chair. Pulled my knees up, trying to
make myself small.

The door to the drop-in center opened and the
guard looked in.

He was an old man, a black guy. A sad face of
hanging flews, like a basset hound. He did not open
the door all the way, but peered in through a crack.
He switched on a flashlight and slowly started to pass
its beam around the room. Over the tatty furniture,
the bulletin boards, the pictures on the wall. Starting
at the far corner. Moving toward me.

I sat there, legs pulled up, eyes pulled wide, my
breath deafening in my ear. I watched as the beam
approached the old armchair that hid me. It gleamed
on it for just a second. It did not hesitate. It passed
on.

I let out a breath of relief. Then the beam hit the
fallen screen.

It stopped. The light held on the screen and I saw
the old guard's eyes narrow. Then the light moved
on. The guard withdrew his head. The door closed
softly.

I grabbed hold of the chair, struggled to my feet. I

stumbled across the room until I fell against the door. I pressed to it, listened through it. I heard the old man's footsteps fading away. I turned the knob and pulled the door open a little. I peeked out.

The hall was empty. The office door on the other side of it was ajar. Light filtered out of it, spilled in a cone across the tiled floor. I heard the plastic clicking of telephone buttons.

I hesitated. One second. Thinking that I might be able to get out now. To make it back to the *Star*. To take my chances with what I had.

But unless I had the story solid, I was through. Bush would suspend me. I'd be unprotected. And there'd be Watts...

I moved out of the drop-in center, crossed the hall to the stairs.

I heard the guard's voice behind me as I started climbing.

"Yes," I heard him say softly. "Right away."

I rose quickly toward the second-story landing. Tried not to think about the hurting as I went. I rose until I was standing in the center of a long carpeted hallway. To my right were two large doors with the word "Cafeteria" stenciled on one of them. To my left, were apartments, two on each wall. I went quietly down the hall toward them.

Scar's was first. There was a white card with his name typed on it in the slot next to the doorframe. That was One-A. One-B was the secretary, Laurie Wilson.

One-C was what I was looking for. The card there

read "Mark Herd." I stopped, took a deep breath. I knocked quietly.

There was no answer. A moment passed. Another. There was no movement from within. I knocked again.

At once, there was a murmur. "What? Who is it?"

"It's me," I said. "Scar."

"Scar?"

"Let me in, man." I knocked again.

"All right. All right. Hold on. Jesus."

I heard him shuffling toward me.

"What do you want? It's almost one."

"Open up."

There was another pause. One breath. Two. Three.

The lock snapped. The chain slid off. The door opened a crack and Mark Herd stuck his head out.

I grabbed the doorknob with one hand. I grabbed his hair with the other. Then I pulled the door shut.

28

The sound of the door slamming into his head was not a pleasant one. Then again, the experience wasn't all bad, either. For one thing, I kind of enjoyed the way his mouth twisted in pain, the way the gasp broke out of it. The way his eyes widened in fear. I could still remember the cold taste of his stiletto.

I pulled the door back, shoved him inside. Followed him into the dark room. He was reeling away from me, clutching his head with both hands. He moaned as he staggered against a chair. Then he tumbled down into it and bent double.

"How did you move the body?" I said. "Come on, punk, I haven't got much time."

But Herd just sat doubled over in the chair, clutching his head. He was wearing a T-shirt and underpants, so I could see the sinews of his arms and legs tightening with pain. To the left, his small bed was a tumble of sheets and blankets. With that and the chair he sat in, there wasn't much room for anything else. The place was no more than a cell, with only a small window looking out over the back garden.

I took a step toward him, as menacing as I knew how.

"How'd you rig the overdose? What'd you use? When did you do it? This is the quiz, son, let's go."

With a roar, he launched himself at me. His arms were knotted. His face was twisted and wild with rage. He was fast and he was strong and he was mean.

But he was young. I stepped to one side and drove my elbow into his temple. He staggered sideways, crashed into the wall. There was a poster hung there, a picture of some scary-looking guy with a guitar. Herd dragged it down with him as he slid to the floor.

"She couldn't have done it alone, Herd. Someone had to help her. What did you do with Mikki Snow's body?"

Slowly, Herd shook his head. He looked up at me from under heavy eyelids. His lips twisted in a sneer.

"You're dead meat," he said.

Then, for a second, there was nothing in my mind but the red heat of rage. The next thing I knew, I had Herd's shirt gripped in my two fists. I had him lifted in the air and I was shoving him against the wall where the poster had been. His head bucked forward and back as I slammed him again and again. I was screaming:

"I'm not guilty, you piece of shit! I'm not going down for this, you hear? You're gonna tell me what happened. Tell me!"

Then there was a powerful arm around my neck. I was being choked, dragged back. I lost my grip on Herd and he toppled to the floor again. I strained against the force that held me. I pulled free. Spun around.

It was Sam Scar.

"Ho! Ho!" he said. "Cool down. You'll kill him!"

He stood poised, waiting to fend me off. He was wearing nothing but trunks, and the black wounds stood out on his muscular arms.

"I got about sixty seconds before the cops get here, Sam. He's gonna talk if I have to rip the words out with my hand."

"Talk what, tell what?"

"He helped Celia Cooper move Mikki Snow's body. He helped her make it look like an overdose."

Herd screamed up at me, the spit flying from his lips. "You stupid shit."

"Leave him alone, Wells," said Celia Cooper. "He had nothing to do with it."

I turned and saw her in the doorway.

She was standing with her arms crossed over her chest, her hands rubbing nervously at her shoulders. In rumpled pants and a billowing sweatshirt, her small thin body looked even more fragile than usual. The weary face looked wearier still. All the same, that aura she gave off, the aura of command—that remained with her. The minute she spoke, Herd, Scar, and I stopped and looked at her and waited for her to speak again.

"Baumgarten called me," she said. "I figured you'd have it worked out by now." She looked down at the floor and shook her head. "Why couldn't you just . . . leave it alone?"

"Because I didn't murder anyone," I said. "And you did."

Her shoulders lifted as she gave a tired laugh. "I wish I had your... simplicity. I wish things were as simple as you think. I never murdered anyone."

"You killed Mikki Snow."

Her eyes flashed up at me. "That was an accident ... that was..." She couldn't hold my stare. "A necessity," she said.

"Because she wouldn't leave it alone either."

"That's right. That's right. And because she was simple, too. Because she thought I was good and that good people do good things and that everything works out for the best and... God knows what else." She let out a long sigh. "And it's not that way, Wells. It's not that way."

"No." I moved to the window. Leaned against the sill. Took out a cigarette. "No, it isn't."

Herd was shifting on the floor now. Massaging the back of his head, trying to bring himself around. Scar moved wearily to the bed. He sank down onto it as if pressed by a great weight. He rubbed his eyes with one large hand.

I lit my cigarette. Celia Cooper and I gazed at each other through the smoke.

"It's all tangled, Wells," she said. "It's all... Ah, I don't know."

"Mikki wanted you to stop, was that it? She wanted you to shut down Baumgarten's money laundry."

She nodded. "And turn him in, too. Not to mention myself in the process. She wanted me to 'clean the corruption out of Cooper House,' she said. 'Make

it what it *should* be.' I tried to explain to her, I tried
to tell her: Nothing is what it should be. There
would *be* no Cooper House after that. Life isn't just a
choice between one thing and another, I told her, we
have to take...what we can. She wouldn't listen.
She yelled at me, called me...names." She paused,
and then repeated it. "She called me names. We
were standing in her office, at the top of the stairs.
The door was open. I'd just come up from the trunk
room and she was there, waiting for me and...the
door was open." Still hugging herself, she leaned
against the doorframe. She stared into the smoky
space between us. "She said she was going to make
sure that justice was done. She said she'd written a
letter, explaining everything, telling everything. To
make sure that justice was done, and she...called
me names. I slapped her. I slapped her, and she fell.
Down the stairs. To the concrete. Her head...she
cracked her head."

Herd moaned from the floor, maybe in pain, maybe in sorrow, I couldn't tell. He rested his elbow on a
raised knee, covered his face with his hand. Scar, his
arms dangling between his legs, stared at the floor
and said nothing.

"How did you know she wrote the letter to me?" I
asked.

"In her..." She had to clear her throat before she
could go on. She kept rubbing her shoulders, as if
she were cold. "In her purse. I found your address. I
guess she got your name from that old story you'd
written about us. We had it tacked up somewhere,
on one of the boards. I don't know why she used your

home address, maybe she thought she was being discreet. I don't..." She shook her head.

"So you got Thad to help you."

She made a vague gesture with her hand. "I didn't know what to do. I was ready to turn myself in, but he said...he said he could hide her. He loved...We loved each other."

"And he'd have done anything to save you."

Her nod was barely perceptible. "He helped me hide Mikki's body in the dumpster. He said he'd find a place to bury her."

"And then he came to get her letter back from me."

Her hands clenched into fists at her shoulders. Her face twisted too as she stared in front of her. "He wasn't supposed to fight with you, he wasn't supposed to do anything like that. He was just supposed to... get it back."

"He found it open," I said. There was an ashtray on the desk behind me. I crushed my cigarette in it. "I'd been about to read my mail the night before, when I got called out on a story. I'd already opened Snow's letter before the phone rang, and I guess I left it lying there. Reich must've just assumed I'd read it and knew everything. He attacked me to protect you."

Her fists sank to her sides. She frowned deeply, as if she might cry. She didn't cry. "And you killed him," she whispered.

"Like you said: there is such a thing as justice."

She came away from the door, stepped into the center of the room. Scar and Herd both lifted their faces to see her. Angry, her mouth tight, her eyes haughty and hot, she was an impressive sight.

"Justice," she said. "That's what you call justice. I've given my life to . . . to helping people, to making things better in this city." She swung a hand at Herd and Scar. "I made their lives better. Thad Reich's. Mikki Snow's. I *gave* her her life—I gave it back to her." She leaned toward me, staring hard. "There are more than a hundred and fifty people housed in this building tonight, Wells. Fed and warm. People who would be on the streets otherwise, or dead. What was Mikki Snow compared to that?" She pulled herself erect. "And what are you?"

Slowly, I came away from the window. I stepped toward her, close to her. We looked at each other, into each other's eyes.

"Not guilty," I said. "I am not guilty."

"Oh!" She leaned back, clapped her hands together so loudly it startled me. "And just what does that mean, what is that supposed to do for you?"

"It gives me the right to be left the fuck alone."

"A small desire for a small man."

"It's funny," I said, "but I don't remember asking your opinion."

I started to move around her.

"Where do you think you're going?"

"To meet the cops. You think a rigged O.D. is gonna hold up once the M.E. knows what to look for?"

I started toward the door.

"Use your head," she snapped. "I never could have fooled the M.E. in the first place."

I was about to step out into the hall—and stopped. Slowly, I turned. She bit her lip, sorry she'd spoken. But there was no show of weakness, no sign that she would waver. She still knew what she had to do.

"Watts," I said.

She didn't answer. I understood.

"And now you've called him. You were down there with the guard when I came in, and you called for Watts."

I looked back at the door to the hall. I could feel the night out there beyond it, the city beyond it, a city of shadows.

"Just give yourself to them," said Celia Cooper. "He'll kill you if you try to run. You know that."

"He'll kill me anyway," I said. "Today or tomorrow. The minute he can." I glanced back at her. "And you know that."

Celia Cooper crossed her arms again, rubbed her shoulders. For a moment, I thought I saw something in those firm eyes of hers, some measure of doubt. But it was gone almost at once.

"It's not just you," she said. "It's not just you and me. Or Mikki Snow or even Thad. I have to think about the greater good, a higher justice."

"Maybe," I told her. "Maybe you do." I headed toward the door again. "But I'll take it one god-damned case at a time."

29

There had been no sirens, but they were out there, all right. I knew it as I moved to the stairs. They were waiting for me to step outside, into the dark. Honest cops, most of them, but with enough of Watts's ringers thrown in to make getting arrested a fatal affair.

I thought of stopping. I thought of grabbing a phone, calling the paper, calling a lawyer, calling Lieutenant Gottlieb to take charge. But I knew if I pulled up, Celia Cooper would start screaming for help. Watts wanted to do it in the dark, but he'd take me wherever he could. I had to get out. I had to get back to the *Star*.

I reached the top of the stairs. Looked down. The old security guard was standing in the hall under the darkened chandelier. He was looking up at me with his hangdog face. He looked sad. He looked sorry for me. I started down toward him.

All around, the house was quiet. I could feel that quiet pressing in on me. I could feel it rolling away from me, too, rolling off into the surrounding night.

I went down the stairs one at a time, my hand on the banister. I looked past the guard to the closed doors, those big wooden doors crisscrossed with iron. I felt my feet touch down on the tiled floor. I felt my heart beating hard, and the sweat gathering on my forehead. I walked across the hall to the door.

I swallowed as my hand wrapped itself around the metal handle. It was cold to the touch. Cold and very real. I pressed the latch, pulled the door. It swung back. The quiet rushed in with the night. The street lay still.

I stepped outside.

I could not see them. Trees lined the sidewalk, blocking the glow of the streetlamps, covering the pavement with shadows. The shadows swayed and shuddered as the trees rustled in the wind. The doorways—to the restaurant's kitchen, to the River City apartments—were completely black. I looked down toward the avenue, then up the hill into the complex. There was nothing moving, nothing at all. I heard the Cooper House door swing shut behind me.

Lansing's car was parked just across the way. The avenue was only a few paces down the hill. If they had left any opening, it would be to my right, up the slope. Maybe they wouldn't be expecting me to go that way.

So I ran. Swiveling to my right without warning. Pushing off with a jump. Pumping my arms, heading for the darkness above me.

"Freeze!"

A cop car, flashers spinning, shot out to block the street ahead.

"Freeze!"

Four silhouetted men stepped out of the shadows to block the sidewalk.

I spun.

"Freeze!"

"Freeze!"

Two more cars, flashing, blocked the road below. More cops poured from the surrounding dark, poured from every direction, closing in on me.

"Freeze!"

"Freeze!"

"Freeze!"

I froze.

"Put your goddamned..."

"Put your hands..."

"Raise your fucking hands over your..."

"Freeze!"

"Put your hands up."

"Don't move, motherfucker."

Slowly, I put my hands over my head, my shaking hands. There was nothing but shouting and my heartbeat and the world gone into the slow motions of absolute fear.

In those slow motions, they kept closing in. They came from behind the trunks of trees, from behind parked cars, from the darkened doorways. They stepped out into the streetlamps' glow, their revolvers glinting in the dim light. Some were in uniforms, one or two were in plainclothes. Their mouths were tight with excitement, their eyes were big with suspense. They held their guns steady. They trained them on me.

And, as the cordon tightened, Lieutenant Tom Watts stepped through it, directly before me. He had his detective special drawn. He held it close to his hip. He pointed it at my middle. Even in the dark, I could see into the endless depths of its black bore.

I looked up into his face. He met my gaze, his green eyes empty of everything but a wild, triumphant gladness.

Then, suddenly, too quickly for me to react, he shouted: "Watch out! He's got a gun!"

He raised his revolver, aimed it at my chest.

There was a white flash. It seemed to burn away everything.

30

"Press!" Lansing shouted. "Press! Press!"

I turned to see her running toward us up the hill, ducking under the low branches. She had her hand in the air. She had her wallet in her hand. She was waving her I.D. card.

"Press!" she yelled. "Press!"

Running just behind her was Gershon, holding his camera up over his head. The strobe waved above it like a periscope. He pressed the shutter release and the strobe sent out that white flash again, burning away the night.

I threw my open hands higher. "I give up!" I screamed. "I'm unarmed! I surrender!"

Watts hesitated—but the moment was past. The strobe kept flashing. Lansing kept running, kept screaming wildly, "Press! Press!" kept waving her card.

Slowly, Watts drew his gun in close to his side. He spat on the ground.

"Get that bitch," he barked. "Grab that camera."

Lansing came to a stop, just outside the circle of police. She leaned forward, panting. Gershon was snapping off pictures even as the cops moved in on him.

"You can take the camera, Watts," Lansing gasped. "But the front page belongs to me."

"You're under arrest," Watts said out of the corner of his mouth. "Interfering with a law officer. Read her her rights."

He was looking only at me, glaring, his gun hand trembling at his side.

Now, though, a patrolman, a kid in his twenties, rushed torward me out of the circle. He grabbed my arm, slapped a handcuff around the wrist. I turned to him and saw a young face alight with hysteria.

"I'm cuffing him!" he shrieked, his voice cracking. "He's cuffed! He's unarmed!" He drew my arms behind my back, linked one to the other. As he did, he whispered, "Hang tough, guy. This mother's nuts."

Watts kept glaring. Even in the half-light, I saw his face darken with the rush of anger.

Below, on the avenue, a new car had pulled up, unmarked, a flasher going behind its windshield. I heard its doors open and shut. I heard another voice coming up the hill, breathless.

"Wait! Wait! I can't run, my heart, there'll be a snap, I'll be gone."

I cast my eyes to a benevolent heaven. "About fucking time," I muttered.

Lieutenant Fred Gottlieb hiked his way out from under the shadows. His round, gristly face was red. There were dark sweat stains on his green paisley shirt and his brown polyester leisure jacket billowed around him.

He slowed down as he edged between the two uniforms who'd closed on Lansing.

"Leave her alone," he said. "She's a nice person, get away from her."

He went past them, huffing up the slope until he stood before Watts. The two lieutenants confronted each other. Watts's lip curled. His finger stroked the trigger of his gun. Gottlieb lowered his head like a bull.

"Fuck off," said Watts. "I'm making a collar."

"Good. You collar," Gottlieb told him. "I'll watch."

They locked eyes another moment. It was Watts who looked away. His mouth was twitching. His triumph and his gladness were all gone.

He managed a nod. More uniforms moved toward me. Two of them grabbed me under the arms.

I spoke up. "Fred."

"Don't start," said Gottlieb.

"There was a body here until this afternoon. A woman named Mikki Snow. Down in the cellar, in a dumpster."

Gottlieb held his hand up. "Wait, wait." The officers relaxed their grips on my arms. "Do you know where it is, this body?"

"Listen, Gottlieb, this is my case . . ." Watts started. Gottlieb spun around on him, without speaking. Watts clamped his shaking lips together.

"This body," Gottlieb asked again. "You know where it is?"

"I think it's still . . ."

"Thinking is not good. Knowing is good."

"I'm pretty sure it's at the morgue, Fred. A woman. They haven't had time to move her. Watts rigged an autopsy with one of the M.E.'s people. Said she was an overdose. But she died of a fall down the cellar stairs right here. At Cooper House."

"This is my collar, Gottlieb," Watts broke in. "If you don't..."

Again, Gottlieb faced him. The silence stretched out between them a long way. Gottlieb's back was to me, but I heard the tightness, the disgust in his voice.

"Cops make collars," he said.

Half of Watts's mouth curled down, his eyes went ugly. Breathing hard, he pulled his overcoat open, baring the holster on his belt. He shoved his gun into the pocket and, with a last glance at Gottlieb— and another at me—he turned on his heel. Back straight, he marched down the hill, vanished into the shadows.

Gottlieb watched him go. His shoulders rose and fell. He glanced at the young cop who'd cuffed me.

"Let him go," he said.

The cop moved around to my back. In a moment, I felt my wrists break free of each other. It felt like coming up after a long time underwater. I breathed like that, raising my face to the sky, taking in great lungfuls of the air.

When I looked down, I saw Lansing coming toward me. Pushing through the cops, stepping close to me. Looking me over as if she hadn't seen me in years. She bit her lip to stop its trembling, but it was no good. Her whole face started to quiver. She came toward me, put her arms over my shoulders, laid her head on my chest, and started to cry.

"Gottlieb," I called, over the top of her. "Get some CSU guys downstairs. As of this afternoon..."

"Hey!" said Gottlieb. He gestured at Lansing. She sobbed into my shirt.

"There were some bloodstains in the dumpster down there," I said.

"Pat her."

"What?"

"On the back. With your hand. You pat her."

I put my hand on Lansing's back. She went on crying.

Disgusted, Gottlieb turned away from me, shaking his head.

"Schmuck," he muttered. "He's such a schmuck."

31

"Fran!" I screamed. "Copy!"

I snatched the page from my typewriter, held it over my head. Fran snatched the sheet as she ran by, screaming, "Incoming! Incoming! Here we go!"

I rolled in a fresh sheet. I clenched my cigarette in my teeth. I squinted through the smoke and started typing again, fast.

"All right, let's do it, get it into the computer," shouted Emma Walsh. She was leaning over Rafferty's shoulder at the city desk. "How much more, Wells?" she called to me.

"Just two graphs. This is the end of it." I kept on typing.

"After this, you're learning the keyboards, you hear me."

"Hold on, I'm writing, this is perky, this is good!"

"It's solid!" Lansing was shouting across the city room. "The M.E.'s making it official."

"All right," murmured Rafferty calmly. "Let's call 'em up and kill the qualifiers."

"Fran!" I screamed. "Copy!"

"Start closing 'em," shouted Emma Walsh.

"Here it comes," yelled Fran. She swept by me as

I pulled the sheet out. She grabbed it from my hand before I could even raise it in the air.

"Is that it?"

"Did you get the confirm into the Watts sidebar?"

"You want more autopsy?"

"Next edition, Lancer."

"Save it for the next edition, Lance, we're done."

"Close 'em up. Let's go."

I leaned back in my chair. I pulled on my cigarette. I sent a stream of smoke up into the city-room fluorescents. I listened to the voices. I felt the hot rhythm of the newsroom beating in me. I felt my own rhythm beating back.

Good copy, I thought. *Good fucking copy.*

"Get the hell into my office," said Emma Walsh.

I sighed. I swiveled around in time to catch the sight of her plaid skirt switching away from me. I tried to stand up. I groaned, sank back into my seat. I tried again and made it this time.

I limped slowly through the maze of the city room. I tried to keep my back straight. It was murder when I didn't. I tried not to bend my knees too much. I tried not to swing my arms. I tried not to let my body know that it was moving.

Emma was already in her office when I got there. When I stepped through the door, she whirled around to face me. She stood beside her desk, her arms crossed under her breasts. Her gray eyes glinted, steely.

"You learn the machines," she said. "You start tomorrow."

"Yeah, tomorrow's kind of a bad day for me . . ."

"I can make it a lot worse." She picked a pencil off

her desk, tossed it back down again. "I mean, you're holding everybody up. That deadline didn't have to be a panic like that. It's ridiculous."

I hung my head in shame. Shuffled my feet, also in shame.

"What the hell is wrong with computers?" she said.

"They give you cancer. And they make these little booping noises. I hate that."

A red flush came into her round cheeks. It was very pretty. I tried to decide whether to tell her that or live to be forty-seven. I waited, silent.

Emma Walsh sighed. She sat down on the edge of her desk. She brushed her long hair back with one hand. "Well," she said. "Aside from that, I'm more or less glad they didn't kill you."

"Thanks."

"That was all Lansing, you know. She had the cops covered every which way. Watts was using land lines, he didn't even put out the call. But there was some backup request at Cooper House or something and she just caught it." She glanced at me sidelong. "She kind of likes you, you know."

"Yeah. Yeah, I know."

She laughed. That pretty, musical sound. "I'm sort of getting used to you myself," she said. Then she stopped laughing, a half-smile on her lips. She just gazed at me. Gazed at me for a long time. After a while, she frowned a little, turned aside. "Whatcha gonna do for my next edition?" she said.

There was an ashtray on Emma's desk. That was new. I dumped my old cigarette into it. Reached into my shirt pocket for another. "Well, I gotta figure how much of the Watts angle I can go with. We won't have Cooper's confession for a while, but we might be able to use my version as part of the story."

"Lay it out."

"Okay. The way I see it, either Watts caught on to the Mikki Snow angle like I did, or Cooper broke down and told him. My guess is she told him. She never really wanted a cover-up in the first place. She was desperate and confused and Reich had convinced her he could save her. When Reich was killed, I think she was ready to give it up. She told Watts the truth and Watts saw a chance to get me. He told her she wouldn't have to go down for the killing if she played along with him, concocted a story they could hang me with. He got her to think about it anyway. And maybe she started to convince herself that it would be wrong for Cooper House to fall apart because of one little mistake. That there was a higher justice at work, and all that stuff. I have a quote on that. Anyway, she stalled for a while. But the body wasn't getting any younger, and once Baumgarten called her and said I was asking around about Snow, once she had Herd confirm I was talking to him—she knew I was closing in. She called Watts and agreed to testify to whatever he said. He took care of the body for her—and put out a warrant for me."

Emma blew out a long breath. "Man oh man. It would've been so much easier if she'd just owned up to it. If she'd just said: 'I've killed someone.' It would've been so much easier."

I turned away from her. "No," I said. I walked

over to the window. "No. That wouldn't have been easy at all."

Emma didn't answer me. I stood in the silence, looked out through the glass. I looked down on Vanderbilt Avenue, Grand Central looming over its sidewalk. The handout truck had arrived with its coffee and doughnuts. It stood parked beside the curb. The line of homeless men and women—ragged, dirty, gray—stretched along the sidewalk for a full block. I watched them. I thought of Cooper House. I thought of Thad Reich.

"John . . ." Emma Walsh began.

But then she stopped as a cheer reached us from the city room. I turned and saw her moving to the door. There was another cheer, applause. I walked across the room and joined her.

We stepped out and looked across the long maze of cubicles. The cheer went up a final time. I saw Lansing.

She was striding toward the city desk. The reporters and editors were moving to surround her. They were clapping, smiling. Some had their fists pumping in the air.

Lansing came on and I watched her. Her long legs flashed from her skirt as she strode. Her blond hair flew out behind. Her hands went up above her head, waving the first hot copy of the bulldog edition.

Its headline read:

JUSTICE!
WELLS IS CLEARED

ABOUT THE AUTHOR

KEITH PETERSON is a journalist living in New York City. Under a pseudonym, he is an Edgar Award-winning author. *The Trapdoor*, his first novel to feature John Wells, was nominated for an Edgar. *Rough Justice* is his fourth John Wells novel. He has just finished work on a film to star Michael Caine.

THE SCARRED MAN

by Keith Peterson

(coming soon from Bantam)

Keith Peterson's four John Wells novels (*The Trapdoor, The Rain, There Fell a Shadow* and *Rough Justice*) have won the young author a broad and devoted readership, critical acclaim and a nomination for Best Paperback Original from the Mystery Writers of America. In *The Scarred Man*, Peterson turns to something a trifle different—a modern ghost story firmly in the mesmerizing tradition of Henry James's *The Turn of the Screw*. Set in a snow-bound Connecticut town at Christmastime, the novel begins with a horror story spun by firelight. Meet Michael North, who soon finds that a fiction casually told is about to change the course of his life. . . .

So then this is what happened on Christmas. First of all there was screaming; laughing, giggling; shouting. Charlie Rose got out of bed early. Photographers covered the event. We staggered out of our room and found McGill amidst a flurry of women. Then the whole pile of us tumbled into the living room. There was some sort of family tradition about having eggs and toast before opening the presents. This we trampled into the dust. Susannah was cooking the eggs and shouting "Wait for me" and running into the living room to yell at us, and then back to the eggs while we tore into our packages. We were animals. I blush to describe the greed.

I gave Charlie an autographed picture of Richard Nixon, which I'd gotten by writing to the guy. He (Charlie, not Nixon) gave me a lighter and a pack of cigarettes, his brand. Susannah came in and I gave her her scarf and I looked in her eyes and I thought about being inside her. She seemed to like it, the scarf. I wish I could've thought of something better.

Then we ate. Then we drank. Then we ate some more. We sat and talked. McGill told stories and everybody laughed. I looked at Susannah and thought about being inside her. Then we ate some more and drank some more and watched the movie *A Christmas Carol* with Alistair Sim on TV and afterward Charlie held forth at great length about why it was better than the Reginald Owen version and the George C. Scott version and possibly the Dickens version and possibly sex and french toast, all of which seemed to be true at the time. We drank and ate and I could have stared at her until I went blind. She had such a goofy smile.

It got dark. I began to think about her leaving tomorrow. Then I didn't think about it. I thought about tonight, when everyone would be asleep except for her and me. It got darker. Charlie built a fire. I watched the fire grow and the orange flames rising. After a while I fell asleep in my chair. We had gone to bed at four A.M., and I was tired. I woke up and Susannah was asleep in her chair and I sat and watched her sleeping. She woke up and she looked at me. It was getting late. They couldn't stay awake forever.

The first one to go was McGill. I was in the kitchen, pouring myself a mug of coffee when he came in to say good night.

"Merry Christmas, buddy," he said.

I nodded. "Thanks for inviting me."

He paused in the doorway. I watched him. I wondered if he knew. He said: "There hasn't been any time to talk."

"Yeah. Christmas," I said.

"Right, right," he muttered. "No time. I had some things . . ." His voice trailed off.

I raised the mug to my lips, touched my lips to the hot coffee, thought of Susannah. "You don't go till February," I said.

For a moment he didn't answer me. He stood in the doorway, his wiry frame bent, his sharp features pointed downward, the kitchen light gleaming in the last gray strands of his hair. Then he looked up quickly, smiled. "Sure," he said. "I'll see you in the morning."

I wandered back into the living room, hoping the others would soon follow McGill's lead. But they were pretty well planted where they were. They sat motionless, black and orange shadows around the fire. No one was even talking anymore. Conversation was dead. No one wanted Christmas day to be over.

I settled into an easy chair again, felt the heat of the fire run up my side, inhaled the steam from my coffee. Looked at Susannah.

"I know!" said Kate suddenly. "We could tell ghost stories. You know: Christmas and the fire and everything."

I didn't groan. It was Charlie.

"Oh hey," he said. "Let's not, okay?"

Kate pouted. "Come on. Why not?"

Charlie puffed up his cheeks and sighed. His sleepy, childlike face glowed in the firelight, looking the soul of mockery.

Angela turned up a corner of her mouth. "Oh, come on, Rose, it might be fun," she said. I knew the battle was lost.

"Oh, man," said Charlie. "I don't know any ghost stories. The only one I know is the 'The Golden Arm.'"

"Ooh, that sounds good, what's that?" said Kate and Kelly and Susannah all at once.

That clinched it. Faced suddenly with the prospect of telling "The Golden Arm" to three attractive girls who'd never heard it before, Charlie was unstoppable. He perked up at once. He rubbed his palms together and chuckled maniacally. I cursed under my breath. Then Charlie launched into it, and I have to hand it to him: Rose rose to the occasion. He told the story as if he'd just made it up. He stood and acted out the husband digging up the wife's body. He crept back to his chair with her golden arm, peering back over his shoulder at the sound of the wind. The wind: he had the eerie howling of it down pat, and you could hear how the wife's voice sort of welled up under it slowly and mingled with it: *"Whoooooo stooooole my gooooooolden aaaaarm?"* When he finally spun on Kate and shouted "You did!" even I jumped in my chair. Splashed coffee down the front of my shirt. And Kate screamed and giggled till I thought we'd have to have her hospitalized.

Charlie sunk his chin on his chest and chuckled. Angela and Susannah laughed. Kelly hugged herself and shivered. It was quiet for a few minutes.

Then Kelly said: "Who else knows one?"

And I heard myself answer: "Okay. I do."

Everybody turned to me. I couldn't believe I had spoken. All I wanted was the quiet of the sleeping house again, the small white feel of her under and around me again. On top of which, Charlie had just told the only ghost story I know. But his performance had inspired me. The little shrieks of the women had gotten my blood up. And so I had spoken, and now there they were staring at me, and I had to say something, fast.

Which is how I came to invent the scarred man.

The moments passed. My mind was blank. I smiled calmly, panicking. Like Charlie, I rubbed my hands together, playing for time. I cast a slow, wicked glance at each of them: Angela with a cigarette held before her lips and her thumbnail pressed to her teeth; Kate and Kelly sitting shoulder to shoulder, two glowing pairs of expectant eyes; Susannah absently rolling the brandy in her snifter around and around;

and even Charlie, perched on the edge of his seat with his arms dangling between his knees—all of them: waiting.

I took a deep breath.

"Okay," I said softly. "Listen."

And I began.

Actually, this story is true [I said] so I don't know if it fits the bill. But it's eerie enough in its way. I heard it from a man named Robert Sinclair, who was once a popular newspaper columnist in Chicago. I met him at a party in SoHo in New York. His heyday was before my time, but I'd heard his name in another connection. Eventually the conversation turned to the old days and his work. Sinclair's primary interest had been crime: He had a lot of good stories to tell and he told them with relish—so much so, in fact, that I eventually asked him why he'd left off doing what he obviously loved. We'd had a few drinks by that time and he seemed ready to tell me, though he gave me a good once-over before he started.

"Are you sure you want to know?" he asked.

I said I was.

"Then I'll tell you," he said. "I'll tell you about the last story I ever covered."

This happened, as I say, before my time, twenty years ago or more, but Sinclair remembered it vividly. At the time it took place he was deeply engrossed in covering the famous Chicago Strangler killings. He was doing the usual profiles of the seven dead women, the police-are-baffled pieces and so on. And what always struck him was that while he was working in the limelight, the story that was to end his newspaper career was beginning in complete obscurity.

In obscurity, it seems, there lived a man named

Honeywell. John Honeywell. In fact, he kept a house in a suburb of the city, but he was obscure enough; a drab sort: quiet, meek; gray. He worked as a book-keeper for a Chicago firm and commuted into the city every day by train. Into the city and out again, that was his life. No wife, no kids, no friends to mention. Like the old song says: nobody knew he was there.

Now, one day Honeywell was riding the train into work—sitting alone, reading his paper—when a man sat down next to him. Honeywell paid no attention to him at first, but after a few moments he became aware of a peculiar smell: a wet, thick, and bitter smell, thoroughly unpleasant. He couldn't help it: He glanced up at the man beside him. There was noth-ing strange about the fellow at all. A medium-sized man in a black suit, white shirt, a thin black tie. Pale face, a thin sharp nose, and close-set blue eyes. Thin blond hair in a widow's peak. As Honeywell glanced at him, the smell grew stronger—and Honeywell, without knowing why, became afraid. And just then the man looked up—looked back at Honeywell—looked him right in the eye. And he smiled. Honeywell wanted to turn away but he couldn't for a moment. For that moment he was mesmerized by the sight of a deep, white, jagged scar that ran from the man's right eye, over his cheek, to the corner of his mouth. The scar seemed to transform the man's whole face— transform it from a nondescript, even pleasant fact, into something horrible. The man's smile seemed almost wicked, and suddenly an odd thought flashed into Honeywell's mind: he thought he knew what that smell was—that smell coming from the scarred man. It was corruption, he thought. It was the smell of evil.

Now, if this were a story, Honeywell would've

gotten up and run away or screamed or something. But in real life you know how it is: He was afraid of being rude, more than anything. He turned away and buried his face in his newspaper—though for the rest of the trip he felt sure the man was still staring at him, still grinning at him—and the smell: he thought the smell would choke him if that ride didn't end soon.

After what seemed a lifetime the train pulled into the station. Honeywell got off and hurried away through the crowd, leaving the scarred man behind him. He went to work and buried himself in his books and figures. He didn't mention the incident to anyone. There had been no incident. And anyway, he had no one to tell. By lunchtime the whole thing seemed to him to have been the product of an overactive imagination.

As the day drew to a close, Honeywell found himself feeling nervous again. He was thinking about the ride home. He stayed longer in the office than usual. In fact, he stayed so long that, when he looked up from his work, he noticed that the building was empty. He sat at his desk, staring out the door of his cubicle on a small section of deserted hallway. Deserted— and silent. So silent that when he heard hollow, echoing footsteps approaching, he gasped. He sat rigid. The footsteps drew closer. And finally, a cleaning woman wandered past. Honeywell seized his briefcase, stood from his desk, and walked swiftly out of the building and into the street.

When he reached the train station, he saw that the rush-hour crowds had thinned out almost to nothing. Honeywell scanned the faces of the remaining commuters carefully as he walked to his train. When he boarded, he made a point of sitting next to another man, though there were still some seats left empty.

All of these precautions, at any rate, were unnecessary. There was no sign of the scarred man.

Honeywell's house was in a pleasantly wooded part of town about ten miles from where the train let him off. He always left his car nearby, so when he arrived in his home station, he went to the car at once and headed off. It was full dark by then, and his drive took him along a curving, unlighted road. He was still a little nervy, and he was in a hurry to get home.

He was about halfway there when it came to him again: that smell, that man's smell. It filled the car, growing stronger and stronger. Honeywell was terrified. He turned his eyes to the rearview mirror, fully expecting the scarred face to appear there like something in a horror movie. He even cast a glance into the backseat. But it was empty. There was only the smell, filling the car, nauseating.

Honeywell rolled down the window. He stepped on the gas. His tires screamed as they took the curves on the road home. By the time his own driveway appeared before him, he was panting, breathing through his mouth, that is, so he wouldn't smell anymore. He came to the driveway. He spun the wheel. The car turned and his headlights swept the darkened drive.

And for one instant, he saw a figure, a silhouette, captured in the beams.

And then the beams passed on and he could see nothing there but the darkness.

Honeywell backed the car up, swept the lights over the spot again. Nothing. But the figure had been there, he was sure of it. He locked all the doors of his car and sat inside, the lights on, the engine on, staring at the door of his house: judging the distance.

Anyone who had been looking on that evening would've then seen a rather comic sight: a mild, gray little man, clutching a briefcase, racing across his own lawn to his own door as if demons were chasing him. When Honeywell got inside, he immediately turned on all the lights. Turned on the TV for company, the radio for good measure. Up until then he had always been very regular in his habits, but tonight his bedtime came and went and he was still seated in his bedroom easy chair, staring at the television. It was past midnight before he could bring himself to go to bed. Even then, he left the TV on and fell asleep to the sound of it.

The tone of the test pattern woke him. The tone—and the smell. His eyes shot open and he sat up in bed—relieved at first to see that dawn was breaking, then sickened to notice that that odor was everywhere in the room. He sat there with the covers clutched to his chin, with all his senses alert. There was no one in the room, and he could hear no one moving in the house. As the light rose outside, Honeywell told himself that, somehow, that man's smell had gotten all over him.

He got up. And he saw the muddy print of a man's shoe on the floor. On the floor right beside his bed, as if someone had been standing over him.

John Honeywell washed and shaved and dressed as fast as he could, and left the house immediately. It was about five-thirty in the morning when he reached the train station. The place was deserted. The ticket office was closed. Honeywell didn't even know when the first train would arrive. He just stood on the empty platform, clutching his briefcase, staring at the tracks, feeling his heart race and thinking over and over again: *What will I do? What will I do? What will I do?*

Then he heard footsteps. They were coming from the covered bridge that went across the tracks. He looked up. The bridge was covered with a kind of pebbled, plastic sheeting, and Honeywell could see the dark figure of a man crossing slowly to his platform. He watched, motionless, as the figure moved to the stairs at the near end. He saw a man's legs begin to descend the stairs. Then his body came into view. And then his face.

It was the scarred man. Coming down the stairs, quietly—inevitably. Honeywell knew there was no sense running or calling out or trying to hide. He could only stand there, as the smell grew thicker, as his heart beat faster—as the scarred man came on, down on the platform now, walking toward him, closer and closer until the smell of him was overpowering and Honeywell's vision was filled with that mild pleasant smile of his, that smile twisted by his scar into something secret and evil. And the man leaned down to Honeywell, so that Honeywell could hardly breathe.

And in a sweet, confidential whisper, the man said: "You."

And Honeywell killed him.

He dropped his briefcase and wrapped his hands around the man's throat and squeezed and squeezed until the man's feet left the ground and he dangled in Honeywell's grip like a rag doll. Honeywell watched, fascinated, as his hands closed tighter with a strength he didn't know he had, as the man's twisted face turned red, then purple, then white, and his tongue fell from his mouth and dangled there as his feet were dangling.

And when the first commuters arrived, they found Honeywell, still there, laughing and laughing, over the mangled body of a woman.

Well, this is where my friend Sinclair comes into it. The police were thrilled to have the Chicago

Strangler case solved, but Sinclair was disturbed by the fact that Honeywell was only charged with one of the eight murders: the last one. Sinclair followed the trial closely, of course. He saw Honeywell's lawyers try to plead their insanity case while saddled with a client who clearly refused to testify. He saw the jury return the only verdict they could—and finally, inevitably, he saw the sentence lowered on the silent, drab little man at the defense table: Death in the electric chair.

A few years later Sinclair managed to arrange an interview with Honeywell and met him for the first time on Death Row. That first meeting made Sinclair come back again—and again. Over a period of time, he gained the little man's confidence and, at last, Honeywell told him the story I've just told you: It hadn't come out at the trial. The story convinced Sinclair of two things: that Honeywell was, in fact, the Chicago Strangler, and that he was, in fact, insane. He began to lobby in his column for the commutation of Honeywell's sentence, and Honeywell began to regard him as his only friend. So when Sinclair finally lost the good fight, Honeywell offered him the one gesture of friendship he had left: He invited him to witness his execution.

Sinclair was there, then, when they led Honeywell into that awful room. The little bookkeeper looked drabber than ever in his death clothes. As the guards strapped him into the electric chair, his eyes darted everywhere as if he were trying to record every impression he could of the last of sweet, terrible life. And then they brought out the hood to put over his head. And Sinclair, looking on through a window, saw a movement behind a partition on the far end of the room. It was the executioner's hand reaching for the switch. Honeywell saw it, too, and he turned toward the motion—saw the man hidden from Sinclair's view—and suddenly shrieked:

"Him! There he is! It's him! It's him!"

The guards had to struggle to pull the hood down over his head. They backed away quickly from the thrashing figure. Then the switch came down. And Honeywell died screaming.

Now, Sinclair could have dismissed even this as madness, if he hadn't attended Honeywell's funeral. Because there, at the graveyard—

"Stop it!"

A glass shattered.

Susannah had leapt to her feet, the brandy snifter falling from her hand. Even in the firelight I could see that the blood had drained completely from her face. She was white. She stood there, looking around at us wildly, her hand at her mouth, her fingers dancing over her lips. Finally her eyes came to rest on me. She stared at me as if I were something risen from the grave.

"What are you doing to me?" she said. Her voice was shrill. "What are you trying to do to me?"

"Susannah!" I was on my feet too. We all were. Kate and Kelly and Angela crowded in around Susannah while Charlie and I looked at each other helplessly.

Susannah began to cry, to sob, her head against Kate's shoulder.

"Make him stop," she kept saying—she said it over and over. "Make him stop it."

Angela turned to me. "Jackass, you frightened her."

I said: "I . . ."

"Look at her, she's terrified."

"I didn't mean . . . I was just . . ." I stepped forward—

and Susannah recoiled from me into the arms of her friends.

"Stay away from me," she said. She was sobbing hysterically now. "Keep him away from me."

"It was only a story," I said. "I made it up. It doesn't even make any sense. There's no Sinclair, no Honeywell. It's all a story."

Susannah eyed me, trembling. "You stay away from me," she said.

Kate said, "Idiot!" And then showed me her back. "Come on, Sue, we'll take you upstairs," she said.

I looked on, helpless, stammering, as the three women led Susannah away. I could still hear her sobbing when they shut the bedroom door.

Special Offer
Buy a Bantam Book
for only 50¢.

Now you can have Bantam's catalog filled with hundreds of titles plus take advantage of our unique and exciting bonus book offer. A special offer which gives you the opportunity to purchase a Bantam book for only 50¢. Here's how!

By ordering any five books at the regular price per order, you can also choose any other single book listed (up to a $5.95 value) for just 50¢. Some restrictions do apply, but for further details why not send for Bantam's catalog of titles today!

Just send us your name and address and we will send you a catalog!